LAPS

RACING ON THE EDGE VOL. 10

SHEY STAHL

USA Today Bestselling Author

Engine/car definitions were used from the following websites:
http://www.empiremagnetics.com/glossary/glossary.htm
http://www.world-sprintcar-guide.com/

Cover Design: Tracy Steeg
Copy Editor: Hot Tree Editing
Proofreaders: Janet Johnson and Barb Nejman
BETA Readers: Lauren Zimmerman and Keisha Todd
Interior Formatting: A Designs

SPEED   ADRENALINE   DESIRE

S H E Y   S T A H L

THE RACING ON THE EDGE SERIES

*A POWERFUL LOVE STORY OF
TRAGEDY, LOVE, AND COMMITMENT.*

DEDICATION

FOR MY *RACING ON THE EDGE* FANS.
THIS BOOK'S FOR YOU.

"THIS MORNING, WITH HER, HAVING COFFEE."

JOHNNY CASH, WHEN ASKED FOR HIS DESCRIPTION OF PARADISE.

PRELUDE–JAMESON

Black Slick – A condition describing a dirt track's surface when it still had enough moisture to keep the material packed, but has hardened and is now taking rubber.

"JAMESON! ARE YOU in here?"

Fuck. Spencer found me.

"Yep."

There went my quiet night.

Taking a deep breath, I prepared myself as my brother approached me. I wasn't the least bit surprised he showed up tonight. Mostly because he'd just found out I bailed his son out of jail and paid off his drug dealer. I had my reasoning behind it, but Spencer didn't always see it the way I did.

"It's always about you. You think the fucking world revolves around you and you can just interfere with everyone. For years I've let you take the lead. When you race, it was always your neck on the line so I stood back and let you do it your way. Well, guess what, Jameson? This is not one of your goddamn races. This is my family. Stay out of it."

Here we were again, arguing about Cole and his stupid-ass decisions but nobody—not even my brother—got away with talking to me like that. Okay, so maybe my mother and Sway, but even then, they'd better have a good fucking excuse.

What Spencer didn't know was how many times I'd bailed his youngest son Cole out of jail. I wasn't about to tell him either. Fuck that.

"He was in trouble and he came to me," I felt the need to tell him.

That was essentially a lie. I hated lying to him, but the truth was Alley was the one who called me and asked me to help.

Spencer may be pissed, but if he knew Alley came to me for help, I had a feeling he would blow a fucking gasket. Mostly because he told both of us to stay out of it.

Get this, I don't listen very well. Surprised? Probably not.

He leveled me a serious look. "I'm not a fucking idiot. I know what's going on. It's my kid, and you need to back the fuck up. For once, this isn't about you," he added. "You can't control *everything*. I told you not to help him anymore."

Did I deserve that? In some ways, yes.

"I mean, fuck, Jameson." Shaking his head, he threw his hands up and began pacing the shop. "When Casten was a kid, he stole cars as a fucking sport." His brow raised. "Did I ever interfere with that? Did I ever tell you how to deal with him or how to punish him? No. I didn't. I stayed out of your kids' lives."

Standing, I buried my hands in the pockets of my jeans. "That's totally different and you know it, Spencer. This wasn't just about me bailing Cole out of jail. He borrowed money from the wrong people. People with connections. If I let him stay there, shit was going to happen. I mean, fuck, man, what was I supposed to do, let them beat the shit out of him and hope he survived?"

Spencer hung his head and then looked back up at me through his dark lashes. It made him look more intimidating that way. Mostly because that was what he was trying to achieve. "You should have come to me."

"And you would have blown up on him and made it worse, or better yet, maybe even ignored it." Shaking my head, my heart pounded as my irritation for the situation amplified. "What the fuck does it matter anyway? It's over and done with, and he's out of trouble. No harm done."

He raised an eyebrow and took a step toward me. I could actually count on one hand the physical arguments Spencer and I have gotten into. It looked to me like I was about to head on over to the other hand. "No harm done? Are you fucking kidding me? You just can't fucking stay out of it, can you? You just can't leave shit alone."

"I get that you're pissed, but back off," I growled, hoping he understood I wasn't fucking around.

"So you bailed him out." He practically spat the words at me. "And what exactly do you see happening now? You think Cole is just gonna see the err of his ways? Fuck, Jameson. Your money can't fix everything. I get it, you've got money, a lot of fucking money and because of that you think you can just buy your way out of everything."

My jaw clenched at the accusation that I just bought my way out of everything. I'd *never* bought my way out of anything.

CHAPTER ONE — JAMESON

*Back Pedaling – Most commonly used in drag racing, the
magical art of the driver easing out of the throttle to regain
traction and avoid or stop tire shake. It's difficult, but the driver
must anticipate the problem and pedal before the car is too far
out of shape, all in less than half a second.*

JANUARY 2027

"**DO YOU THINK** he's nervous?"

Nervous? That was actually laughable.

I raised my eyebrows. "His girlfriend's pregnant, and this is the
first big race since he was, like eleven. What do you think?"

"I guess you're right." Tommy smiled at me, his luminous eyes
brightened by the lights wrinkled at the edges. "He's totally fucking
calm."

Shaking my head, I watched Casten a little closer as she held
Hayden's hand in the pits of the Chili Bowl. It was different seeing
him here, not only with a girl but racing. When Ryder died, Casten
quit racing altogether without a second thought. Wouldn't even step
foot in a car.

I understood why he walked away, and I understood in every
way why he returned. Racing was a way of life. You couldn't walk
away from it and say to yourself, I'm never going back. It didn't work

that way. Not when you'd been around it your entire life like our family had.

Sway approached me, her arms wrapping around my waist as she leaned into my back. "They look so cute together," Sway noted, giving a nod to Casten and Hayden.

Tossing her a wink, I asked, "Remember your first time at this race?"

Blinking slowly, her cheeks warmed. "I do. I remember thinking to myself, holy shit, I need to up my whore game if I'm going to keep his attention."

Raising an eyebrow at her, I shook my head. "You were the only one I wanted."

"Technically, that's not true, but are you feeling okay?"

"Yeah, why?"

"You're being nice. Usually you're moody before a race."

"It feels good to be here with you guys."

"You always hoped he'd come back to racing, didn't you?"

"I did. I'm proud of him."

To our left, Tommy walked back over to me with my helmet. Sway smiled as if she knew something was up. "Why do you have Jameson's helmet?"

"That's a good fucking question. Why do you have it?"

"We chubbed it for good luck." Tommy actually looked fucking proud as he said that.

"What the fuck is chubbed it?" Stepping toward him, his face paled. "And who is *we*?"

"You know,"—he grabbed his crotch with his right hand and cupped his junk—"rubbed our dicks on it. Me, Willie, Logan... a few others."

I'm going to be sick. Right after I fucking kill him. And they thought I'd wear it after that? *Yep, I could feel the vomit rising.*

Sway pointed in my face. "Don't you dare throw up. Be a man."

Be a man? Was she serious?

All the blood left my head. My face had to be white. Pure fucking white and fuck if I wasn't starting to sweat.

Sway looked at me, concerned. Her brow furrowed. "Jameson, you're pale."

I look at her, stunned. After all these years did she not know me? Of course I was fucking pale. Those asswipes rubbed their dicks on my helmet. Their DICKS.

It was a constant battle between me and the guys of JAR Racing to play pranks on one another. To me, this was crossing the line. Mostly because I hadn't thought of this one yet and they one-upped me for the weekend. *Fuckers.*

Sway took the helmet from Tommy and moved to stand between us as she placed her hand on my chest right before I lunged for him. "If you know what's best for you, fire crotch, I'd run far away. Maybe even outside the building."

Tommy may be a dumbass on a regular basis, but even he knew good advice when he heard it. The asshole took off, laughing all the way.

"You better fucking run!" I yelled after him. And then I looked at Sway, glared actually. "Can you fucking believe them?"

She rolled her eyes at me as if my anger wasn't warranted, shaking her head. "I don't see why you're surprised at all. You left your helmet in the hauler, dumbass. Clearly one of them was going to mess with it. Just be glad it wasn't glitter this time." She began walking away. "Remember, you got an eye infection from the glitter?"

I hadn't forgotten that one. I still had a spec of glitter in my left eye that had been there for years.

I kept pace with her as we headed back to the hauler, darting in and out of the crowds. "And what do you think their dicks have on them? I need a new helmet." There was absolutely no way I was putting *that* helmet on. I was going to burn it.

"You do not and there's no time. You left your spare at the hotel and the main starts in twenty minutes. I wouldn't have enough time to get to the hotel and back to get the one you left there."

Man, she's really domineering and moody tonight. Fuck if it wasn't turning me on.

"I can't believe you would think I would wear a helmet they put their dicks on," I pointed out to her when we reached the hauler. Casten and Axel stood there with Jack and Jonah beside them.

"What's a dick?" Jack asked curiously. He looked up at me, waiting for an explanation.

I turned to Axel. "You explain that one. I have to find a new helmet."

"Well, Jack,"—Casten wrapped his arm around him, his voice taking on a diplomatic approach—"it's a man's—"

He clearly didn't finish before Axel's hand flew over, smacking him in the ear. "Shut the fuck up, man. The last thing I need is him telling Lily. She's already pissed at me tonight."

Casten shoved Axel's hand away rubbing his ear. "Dammit! What's with this family and smacking me in the ear? Besides, when is she not mad at you?"

Just then the horn sounded for the drivers to get to their cars. Sighing, I looked down at my helmet. I would steal someone else's. That was all there was to it. No fucking way I was wearing this one.

Tossing it inside the hauler, I grabbed Justin's off the counter. He didn't make the main, so it wasn't like he needed it, right?

Only Justin stared at me once I was by my car as I held it up in the air. "Hey, man, do you mind if I borrow your helmet?"

"Why do you need my helmet? What happened to yours?" The look he gave me was more amusement than curiosity.

"Tommy and Willie rubbed their dicks on mine."

That was all I had to say before his face screwed up in horror. "What the fuck?" He looked as if he was going to throw up and I'd be right there with him. "Yeah, take mine, dude." And then he was quick to add, "If they ever chub mine, I'm gonna kill 'em."

How did I not know what chubbed meant until ten minutes ago? "Yeah, well, I'm still thinking about it."

ONCE I WAS inside my car for the race, I kinda forgot about the chubbing incident. Racing had a way of doing that to me. It was my fifth year straight racing in the Chili Bowl. I always enjoyed it mostly because it was a chance to get back to what started my love affair with racing.

Midgets.

During the pace laps, I was calm, as always, but it threw me a little seeing Casten and Axel in the same race.

The race was much like any other midget race, and while I definitely preferred sprints to midgets, it was still fun. Axel was a man on a mission and came out of nowhere in those final laps passing me on the inside. I knew his driving style; he never passed on the inside.

Never.

But he did, and I couldn't be happier he pulled that move. I managed to snag a second place finish with Casten behind me right on my ass.

Tears formed in my eyes seeing my boys in the victory lane together. "I can't even begin to tell you how proud I am of you two."

They'd never understand this feeling; I was sure of it. I thought of my dad right then, the tears burning more and what he'd said to me when I won my first Cup race.

"Nothing in the world can come close to seeing you live this dream of yours."

I finally understood that.

"He'd be proud right now," Tommy noted, wrapping his arm around me. Figured he would know what I was thinking.

"He would be." It was an emotional moment for all of us.

Until Tommy said, "Sorry about rubbing my dick on your helmet."

I gave a nod to victory lane. "Carry me and I'll think about forgiving you."

I had at least twenty pounds on Tommy. Maybe thirty.

"I think I threw my back out."

"I hope you broke it," I flat out told him, picking myself up off the ground.

"You don't mean that," he groaned, rolling onto his back on the concrete. His arms flopped over his face.

"Pretty sure I do." I kicked his thigh. "You chubbed my fucking helmet."

"That was hours ago. Let it go already."

"What's wrong with him?" Casten asked, standing with a beer in his hand, his arm around Hayden as they celebrated in victory lane.

I gave the bottle of muscle relaxers Tommy had to Casten. He had so many back problems that Tommy literally kept his muscle relaxers on him. "Keep the bottle. He'll take the whole damn thing if you don't watch him with it."

"**SO I TAKE** it that helmet isn't going in the showroom?" Sway asked, gesturing to my helmet in the back of the truck. I refused to put it inside with us.

"Not a chance. I'm burning it."

Sway and I were in the truck on the way back to the hotel that night when Casten called.

"We have a *problem*," he said immediately. Casten downplayed everything. Someone could be dying and I swear he'd tell me it was a scratch. So for him to say, there was a problem, something was wrong.

"Why am I not surprised by that?"

"Shut up. Tommy took like six muscle relaxers." I groaned just at those words, knowing damn well what happened.

Tommy threw his back out giving me a piggyback ride after the race. In hindsight, it probably wasn't the best idea we'd had, but screw the fucker. Served him right.

As far as I was concerned, Tommy could die and I wouldn't give any fucks about it. Okay, that wasn't entirely true, but he did rub his dick on my helmet so I wouldn't care as much. "I told you not to let him have the bottle."

"I didn't." And then he was silent as I heard screaming in the background. "Fuck, I gotta go, Dad. Come to the hospital. Hayden's in labor."

Dropping my phone onto the center console, I turned around and headed in the direction of the hospital, laughing. I almost feel bad for the kid.

"What's so funny?" Sway asked, smiling over at me.

"Hayden's in labor."

"Really?"

"Yeah, and apparently Tommy took a bunch of muscle relaxers." At a stop light, I looked over at her. "He's an idiot. If it wasn't for us, he'd be dead already."

"Remember the time when he ate that entire chocolate laxative bar?"

I cringed remembering that day. "I try not to."

The drive to the hospital was quick. Walking up to the emergency room doors, Sway was digging in her purse mumbling about finding her damn phone so she could take pictures as soon as the baby was born and talking about hoping it was a girl. "I just really want a granddaughter."

"You have a daughter. I don't see what the big deal is."

"It's different. And Arie never liked me much."

"That's not true and you know it."

Looking down and shaking my head, I couldn't help but chuckle because I couldn't understand why anyone would want any pictures of a baby as soon as it was born. I didn't care what anybody said, babies are not cute as soon as they were born. They were the opposite actually. Covered in goo and shit. No. Not cute.

Still laughing to myself, Sway swatted my stomach with her hand, forcing me to stop.

Rubbing my stomach, I stared at her. "What the hell? Stop hitting me."

She quickly covered my mouth with her hand. "Shut up. Look over there."

I turned to where she was pointing and a huge grin spread across my face. All those times Casten pulled shit and got off with his smile or some stupid fucking excuse, well, it was all coming around.

We arrived there just in time to see Tommy piss on Hayden. Yes, piss right on her leg.

"I've seen Tommy's dick too many times in my life." Sway refused to look up.

"You motherfucker!" Hayden yelled at Tommy. Casten stared at Tommy as if to say, really, dude, but it was clear he was starting to lose control.

Tommy giggled, buttoning his pants and leaning against Willie. "Careful there, my dick's like a fire hose. Once it gets to swinging, you never know where it's going."

"Damn. And our parents thought we were a shit show when we had Axel." Sway tugged on my arm. "Come on. We better help Casten before Hayden kills Tommy while giving birth in the emergency lane."

As we approached, Casten finally saw us. The look of relief spreading across his face almost made me feel bad for the asshole.

"Thank fuck," he breathed, hugging his mother. "Can you please take Hayden into the hospital while I deal with Tommy?" His eyes pleaded and of course, that was all it took for Sway to kick in to save her baby boy. She had always been a sucker for him.

"Sure, honey. We'll take care of everything. You just deal with that mess and we'll see you inside."

Once everything inside began to calm down, Tommy was wheeled away, and Hayden was admitted and placed in a birthing room. That left me in the waiting room trying to find a comfortable chair with my iPad.

About fifteen minutes into whatever the hell was playing on the television, Sway walked out of Hayden's room and sat down next to me. "You wanna go in there?"

"Nope." I scrolled through posts on Twitter about the race, seeing if anyone had anything good to say. "Got no desire to see that. Let me know when the kid is here." She stood up rolling her eyes, and as she started to walk away, I grabbed her hand. "Hey, wait, get me some Skittles."

"No. You get them."

Sticking my bottom lip out, I tried to look innocent. "You're being mean to me."

She waved me off. "Oh, stop."

The look didn't work very often, but I still tried every chance I could.

As she walked into the room, I couldn't help but watch her ass in those jeans. My wife would always have the best ass around as far as I was concerned. Mostly because women tended to think they need to fit into a size two. I didn't think Sway had been a size two since high school and I fucking loved that. She was a real woman.

A few minutes later a nurse came around the corner wheeling Tommy toward the waiting room. He was hooked up to an IV and had a smile on his face.

"What the hell are you doing here?" I barked at him because I wasn't happy with him. You didn't forgive someone for rubbing their dick on your helmet in just a few hours. No. Not okay at all.

"Why are you so mean to me? I'm sick." He then lifted his arms to show me his IV like that meant shit to me.

"You're not sick. You're stupid. *Big* difference." Looking over at him, he sat there giggling at his phone. *See? Stupid.* There was no way I was gonna sit out here and babysit this shithead. I would make Casten deal with him.

Yes, brilliant idea.

Once I wheeled Tommy into the room and ran, I wandered the halls looking for a damn vending machine that had Skittles, giving myself a mental fist pump for getting away before anyone could catch me and make me take him back.

Once I found the vending machine, I returned to the waiting room hoping I didn't find Tommy sitting there like an asshole waiting for me.

When I said it was going to be a long night, I sure as hell knew what I was talking about. It took for fucking ever. Between Hayden's screams and Tommy's crying, it seemed like the baby would never get here. By the time the baby was finally born, I was as relieved as Hayden.

Gray Marie Riley. I had a little granddaughter, and they named her Gray after Grays Harbor. The moment they told us her name Sway immediately cried. The fact that Casten wanted to honor us was nearly mind blowing for me. The kid used every opportunity to piss me off and now here he was being nice. Go figure.

As I looked down into my granddaughter's tiny face, I realized I was wrong earlier. Maybe not all babies were cute right when they are born, but this baby, my Gray, she was beautiful.

"She looks just like you both," Sway sighed, hugging Hayden as he held the baby.

As Casten and Hayden talked about her never wanting to have another one, I kissed Hayden's forehead. "Give me my granddaughter. It's time I held her."

I'd had different connections with all my grandkids, mostly when they were old enough to actually interact with me, but with Jack, and it seemed Gray, there was something different. With Jack, he was the first grandkid, and I instantly had a connection to him in that way. Jonah and Jacen too, but I didn't see them as much as I saw Jack.

"She's pretty." I winked at Hayden. "Just like her mama."

Sway burst into tears beside me, her chin resting on my shoulder as she watched me holding her. I sighed and whispered, "You're a mess, honey," to her.

"I know," she breathed out, using my shoulder to wipe her tears.

Laughing lightly, my eyes dropped to Gray as she slept quietly in my arms. I knew this love would be different. My first granddaughter.

I thought back to when Arie was born, and I held her for the first time, knowing I'd never deny her of anything and protect her.

ONCE ALL THE excitement died down, Sway and I headed back to the hotel to finally get some sleep and to allow Casten and Hayden to enjoy their first night as a family.

"You're not tired are you?" I asked, leaning into the doorframe much like I did that night in Charlotte when I asked her to stay. Only this time I wasn't drunk and laying on my back on the floor. For some reason, and maybe it was because of being in victory lane with our boys, but I had been reminded of that night a lot tonight.

"Get over here, Sway!"

Her eyes lit up in a way I'd never seen before, wrapping her arms around my waist.

"I'm so proud of you," she whispered, searching my eyes.

For a moment, it seemed as though she could feel everything I was feeling.

With a look of amusement, Sway stared at me as I pulled my shirt over my head and tossed it on the bed. "Can we make another baby?"

Okay, well the look was one of amusement so I assumed she was referring to us doing a little align boring. Which I was all for. Believe it or not, the adrenaline from the race was still with me a little. "We can try—"

"No, I mean *actually* have another one," Sway clarified, watching my facial expressions closely.

She wasn't serious, was she? I did that thing where my mouth moved a couple times, and no words came out. And then I finally said, "I had a vasectomy."

"Get it reversed."

"Why?" The fuck I would. Nobody would ever take a knife near my balls again.

"Because I want another baby." *Yep, she's serious.*

Brushing her hair off her shoulder, I cupped her cheek tenderly. "Did you hit your head tonight?" I was a little sterner when her facial expression remained the same. "No fucking way. Look at our children."

"What about them? I just watched our youngest become a father."

I gazed at her in complete disbelief. "Which is exactly why we shouldn't have another one. We're grandparents for Christ's sake."

Tears formed in her eyes. "Well, can we at least pretend to make one?"

That's what I'm talking about.

I started ripping off my clothes before she said *pretend* and by *one*, I was naked.

"Well,"—she came to stand in front of me, her hands on my bare shoulders—"you're eager, aren't you?"

"I am. Now,"—I turned her so she was facing the window of the hotel room and then proceeded to take off her shirt in front of the window—"let me remind you of the benefits of not having babies anymore." Dipping my head forward, I kissed her left shoulder and then ran my lips across her shoulders. Taking each one of her hands, I placed them flat on the window. "We can fuck, whenever, and wherever we want...."

"I like where this is going." Sway moved her leg to the window sill. "Fuck me in front of this window."

"Well, take your damn clothes off then."

She looked over her shoulder at me expectantly. "Dude, that's your job."

My gaze lowered, as did my voice. "Yes, it is." I knew then what she wanted. Sway wanted to feel younger. It happened with age and I totally understood it. So why not give her the little dirty heathen she craved every once in a while, right?

This would require ripping panties off like I used to and showing her just how badly I wanted her. And luckily, for her, I was just the man for the job.

"I want the dirty heathen," she whispered.

Every time I was with Sway, I was utterly incapable of going slow or taking my time. I did, but it wasn't without effort. She was just that fucking sexy.

"Is that so?" Taking a fist full of her panties, I yanked once, barely registering the sound of fabric tearing. "Is this what you want?" I asked, my lips brushing over her shoulders. Grabbing a handful of her dark hair, I tugged backward until her head rested on my shoulder where I kissed the side of her face.

Parting her lips, she raised up on her tiptoes to align her pelvis with mine. "Yes," she gasped softly, turning to kiss me, my lips exploring her soft skin.

Standing behind her, I spread her legs running my hands over her hips as I ground myself into her ass. Forcing her lips open with my tongue, I deepened the kiss, her succumbing to the forceful domination of mine.

My free hand roamed intimately over her breast, worshiping her body in all the ways I needed to. The feel of her around me was almost painfully intense, but better than anything.

Sway had other ideas and was frustrated at my slow speed. "Dude, I said fuck me in front of a window, not stand there." She slapped my shoulder. "Get to work."

Arching her back against me suddenly, forcing us together deeply. It was my turn to gasp at the flood of sensations.

A heady groan ripped through my chest. "Stop hitting me, woman," I growled, slamming into her, my hand slipping out of her hair and onto her hip.

"Hey, look, Justin and Ami are down there in the pool." With her hands splayed out on the floor-to-ceiling window, she peered down out of the four-story window. "I'm pretty sure they can see us down there."

"Probably." Reaching up, I put my hand on the back of her neck, her face pressing into the window. "No talking." With the idea of an illicit fuck against a window, the pressure deep in the pit of my stomach built quickly.

I wasn't lasting long, but I took comfort in knowing I would be ready again within minutes.

I wouldn't finish without her, though. I wouldn't take this much pleasure from her body and not give back. Reaching between us, circling the spot I knew so well. It took under a minute for her to fall apart against the window.

Watching Sway in the midst of her orgasm was both a beautiful and fascinating sight. It quickly became my own breaking point; I couldn't stop.

When I could think and move again, I collapsed against her.

"Okay, now they really can see us." She motioned to someone below, clapping.

I laughed, stepping back. "I guess so."

We had just untangled ourselves and stepped away from the window when my phone chirped with a message.

"Justin says thanks for the show," I told Sway, preparing to be hit as I set my phone down.

Sway punched my shoulder as she passed by me toward the shower. "You fucker. I told you they could see."

Laughing, I rubbed the spot she hit. "My bad."

STAHL

CHAPTER TWO —JAMESON

Attenuator – A device mounted at the rear of an IRL car to absorb impacts to the rear end.

DECEMBER 2027

"**WHY DO I** have to go? I mean, can't we just cancel it?"

"Jameson, it's *your* company's fucking Christmas party. JAR Racing is literally your name. Stop being such an asshole and just deal with it."

"It's bullshit," I grumbled with sarcasm. "I don't know why we keep having these damn parties. It's the same stupid shit every year. Tommy, Willie, and Dave get wasted and do something incredibly fucking stupid that they think is hilarious or brilliant. Most of the night is spent with me talking the cops out of arresting their asses."

Annoyance hovered in her stare, and I knew she was about to lay into me. "Yeah, well, I can remember quite a few years where I spent most of my night talking the cops out of dragging your ass to jail so don't be a hypocrite."

Shit. She's right.

"Whatever." My gaze moved out the window to our backyard. "All I'm saying is I don't think it's necessary for *me* to go to this party. I could stay home. No one is even going to notice if I'm there or not."

Her lips puckered, looking at me in disbelief. "*Everyone* is going to notice if you're not there so quit your bitching. Stop sulking. You're going."

I scoffed at her accusation "Sulking? I'm not sulking. I'm contemplating."

Contemplating how to fake a sickness.

Reaching out, she patted my head like I was some fucking dog. "Sure you are, honey."

I was done talking about it. All it did was raise my blood pressure and piss me off. I just didn't like Christmas parties and everything that went with them. I'd much rather stay at home and be with my wife alone. Was that too much to ask?

Apparently so if you asked my family.

Stirring my coffee, I watched Sway pouring coconut creamer in hers. "Do you want some coffee with your cream?"

"Shut up." Placing the creamer back in the fridge, she eyed me, her lips thinned with irritation. "Why are you being mean this morning?"

"I'm not being mean just making an observation. You use way too much creamer. Do you even like the taste of coffee?"

"No, as a matter of fact, I don't, but I also don't see what that has to do with anything. Nobody likes the taste of coffee. It's a necessary evil in my life and I may as well enjoy it."

I raised my eyebrows at this statement because seriously? "*I* like the taste of coffee."

She sat down on my lap, refusing to sit in her own chair at the table. "Yeah well, good for you."

"Now who's being mean?"

Sway turned to give me her full attention. "Look, Jameson, I'm about to go to a doctor's appointment where I have to basically get naked and be felt up. Not to mention he is going to stick a giant Q-tip in my vagina and a finger up my ass."

The fuck? "What do you mean a finger up your ass?"

Apparently, it was a stupid question because Sway rolled her eyes and turned back to her coffee before we had to leave. "Seriously, what do you think goes on at these appointments?" she finally asked.

"Not that. I'm actually a little upset they stick something in your ass. How invasive."

I wasn't sure what I thought happened when Sway went to the lady doctor, but I could tell you it would have never included a finger entering anyone's asshole. Just the thought made me shudder.

"Oh yeah? What exactly goes on at your appointments?"

I stood, pushing her off my lap. "We're most certainly *not* talking about those appointments."

As far as I was concerned, those appointments weren't going to happen for me. I was too young for that still, and if I didn't talk about it, it wouldn't happen.

I DIDN'T THINK much of it that morning. Routine doctor's visit, right? She had them every year. The only difference is, this time, I went with her because I had a meeting in Charlotte anyway.

The thing with routine was that everyone's routine was different. Because of Sway's family history with cancer her routine exam usually meant that they would perform a breast exam, have a mammogram and then if they saw anything suspicious, they would biopsy it just to make sure it was nothing serious. This was a cycle we had gotten used to. I figured today wouldn't be any different. Just another day in our routine.

Wrong.

Very wrong.

During Sway's exam, Dr. Keegan found a lump he wanted to follow up with quickly.

Sway was given an appointment for a mammogram that same day. Still, we didn't think anything of it.

The day after, Friday morning, and I remember the date specifically, December fourteenth. The mammogram office called and scheduled Sway for a biopsy Monday morning in Charlotte. While I wasn't happy about her having to go through another biopsy, I wasn't worried either. Like I said, everyone's routine was different, and we had been through this before. Everything would be fine.

Monday morning came and we were out of there in less than an hour. When Dr. Keegan's office called back that same afternoon and asked us to come in to go over Sway's biopsy results, I knew something wasn't right. Sway knew it too. I could see it in her eyes. It was like she expected this call would come someday.

Hell, in some ways, I was sure she'd prepared herself for it to come.

Sitting in the doctor's office, hearing him go over the results and explain what they meant, it was as if my whole world tilted. I fucking knew how true the statement that your life could change on you in an instant was. You could be running the high line flying past everyone and catch the brim, and you were done. Tire shredded, car all smashed to shit and out of the race. There went your perfect season.

That was exactly my thought hearing the word cancer.

Fucking cancer. I repeated it in my head a few times, trying to process it.

It was like a bad slow-motion wreck. You could see what was going to happen, saw the wall coming full speed, but you couldn't do anything to stop it. You just had to wait and hope there would be something left after the impact.

Dr. Keegan's voice snapped me out of my thoughts. "I know this is scary, but we have a lot of options right now," he went on to say. "You're Stage two, which means while the cancer is slightly more advanced than Stage one it has stayed contained within the breast."

I looked at Sway, who sat stick straight like a statue without the slightest twitch. "What do we do now?" she asked, reaching for my hand.

It seemed like a simple question, but we both knew the answer was going to be anything but simple.

The doctor drew in a deep breath and walked around to the front of his desk placing himself directly in front of Sway. "Well, right now we wait."

Wait? He can't be serious.

She stared up at him, and that was when I freaked out. Naturally. Waiting wasn't something I was okay with. I mean, fuck, she had cancer. *Get it out. Do something. Don't wait for it to kill her.*

"Wait? What the fuck do you mean wait?" I leaned forward, my hands shaking as I let go of Sway's hand. "You just told us that my wife has cancer and now you're telling us to wait." With my heart pounding, my chest aching as the adrenaline coursed through me, I was losing control.

"Well, like I said, with Sway being stage two we have more options because the cancer hasn't spread to other parts of her body.

I'm going to give you recommendations for Oncologists. Doctors I would trust with my own family and once you choose who you want to meet with, they can give a more in depth explanation of your choices."

That's it. Just wait and see what happens?

I wanted to rush her to the hospital and make them take it out like it was an abscessed tooth or something. I was sure if we acted straightaway, like that very second, it would be over.

The truth was, I knew what this meant. Despite everything from plane crashes to parents dying, we hadn't been tested like this. Not yet at least. We were about to find out just how far we could be tested before we broke.

Right then, staring at my wife as a tear slipped down her cheek, her eyes already taking on a sense of regret, I knew then I'd do anything, fight harder than she ever thought possible to save her.

I had to.

Jumping out of my chair, I paced the small room, running my hands through my hair in total frustration.

"No." I shook my head violently back and forth. "That's not good enough. We need to do something now. Right now. Call someone." The unevenness in my voice echoed through the room, settled in my head, a reminder of the fragile edge I was hanging onto.

I faced the doctor, my fists clenching, rage boiling below the surface. "I mean what fucking good are you if you can't help us? What kind of goddamn doctor are you to sit here and tell us to wait? She has cancer, not some goddamn hangnail!" Sway looked at me in horror, her hand covering her mouth, but I was too far gone. There was no turning back for me.

With what resembled an entire body shake, my rage was almost overwhelming. Turning toward the chair I had been sitting in just moments ago, I kicked it across the room before I turned and punched the wall holding all of his useless fucking diplomas. Pieces of paper that didn't mean shit when it came down to it because all he could tell us to do was wait.

"FUCK!" I screamed as I rushed out of the office and down the hallway toward the exit. I didn't even know where I was going, just that I couldn't breathe, and I had to get out.

"Jameson!" The desperation in Sway's voice stopped me in my tracks. When I glanced at her, because I couldn't ignore the tone of her voice, I gasped. Shit. *How much of a selfish bastard can I be?* I was losing my mind, yelling and kicking chairs, when it was *her* that should be falling apart.

I took a minute to catch my breath, and when I turned around seeing the look of devastation in her eyes, it hit me right in the chest like a hammer. Tears steadily streamed down her cheeks. It was all I could do to get to her fast enough to wrap her in my arms and hold her tight. "I'm so sorry, honey." I couldn't hold her tight enough as I kissed her forehead.

"It's okay. I get it. It's a lot to take in." She drew back, examining my face. Raising my hand, I went to brush my palm over her cheek. Only it was bleeding so I dropped to my side. "I actually would have been worried if you didn't punch something." A sad smile took over, wiping away the tears from her cheeks. "Let's just go home and we can talk about things then."

ONCE WE WERE back in the truck, the ride home was long. Neither of us said a word. I was looking ahead holding onto the steering wheel so hard I could have sworn it started to bend, and Sway sat with her hands in her lap staring out the window. I would turn to look at her every few minutes, and it was obvious she wasn't actually looking at anything. She was lost in her own thoughts.

I couldn't imagine what must have been going through her mind. I knew being diagnosed with the same disease that robbed her of her mother at such a young age was one of her greatest fears.

Pulling into our driveway, I noticed everyone seemed to be enjoying our house when we weren't even fucking around. Parked in the driveway were Tommy's Firebird and Willie's truck, which was the last fucking thing I needed.

Throwing the truck into park, I was ready to storm into the house and tell them to get the fuck out. Only Sway grabbed my hand and my attention.

"Leave them. It'll be nice to have a distraction," she told me looking out the window toward the house.

She was right. With them in there, more than likely it would be entertaining.

Taking a deep breath, I eased back into my seat and shut the door. "Are we gonna tell them?"

Immediately, as if she didn't have to think about it, she shook her head. "No. Not yet." Turning back to watch my face, her tears slid down her cheeks. "Growing up I never understood why my parents made the choices they made when it came to telling me when they were sick. I couldn't understand how they could let me go on thinking life was good when they were struggling to live." Pausing, she drew in a shaking breath and reached for my hand. "But I get it now. I get how they wanted to protect me for as long as they could." Her eyes were distant, thinking of the kids I supposed. "I don't want them to know yet. I don't want to be the one to turn their world upside down today. Once we know what we are truly facing, once we know what our options are and what our choices will be, then we'll tell them. But not now." She squeezed my hand. "Let's just let them believe that everything is fine until it's not."

This woman. This was why I married her, for what she was inside. No matter what she was facing, she would always put her family first.

"Okay, honey. Whatever you want." Giving her hand one more squeeze, I leaned in and kissed her cheek softly and opened the door to my truck.

Taking a deep breath, I reminded myself I had to keep it together for Sway. I tried to clear my mind as I rounded the truck to reach her hand, but it was a struggle I wasn't sure I could keep up with.

Sway glanced down at our clasped hands and then back up at me with a soft smile. "We got this, Jameson. You and me. We got this."

I hoped to hell she was right.

CHAPTER THREE —SWAY

Billet – Raw material form of forged metal that can be machined.

CANCER.

Such an ugly, life-altering word.

I knew eventually this day would come. How could it not? Both my parents died at a young age from cancer. My mother from breast cancer when she was twenty-five. Her mother when she was fifty-three. I had just sorta told myself it would or could happen. Had I jinxed myself into it? Some kind of crazy brain effect?

The possibility of breast cancer weighed heavily on me the older I got. For this reason, I'd had mammograms every year since I was twenty-five.

As I stared at the pamphlet and the oncologist's name on it, I knew it had become our reality.

Jameson stared straight ahead, his eyes on the road as we drove from Charlotte back to Mooresville. Watching him carefully, I wanted to know what he was thinking. He said nothing in the doctor's office. Hell, at the time, I wasn't even sure he had been breathing. He was so still, blinking slowly, but I saw his knuckles turn white as he gripped his chair and the way his breathing faltered.

"Say something," I finally breathed out, desperately needing to know his thoughts.

For a moment, he remained quiet until his right hand slipped off the steering wheel and to my thigh. "I love you."

Smiling, I placed my hand over his and squeezed. "I mean about what the doctor said."

Again, he was quiet until he glanced over at me a few minutes later. "I...." His voice shook around the word. He was near tears. "I'm not sure I have words right now." And though the tears in his eyes didn't fall, I knew it wasn't without effort.

"**YOU'RE A REAL** cockbag," Tommy said to Willie when we came inside the house after being gone most of the day.

Rosa, Tommy, Willie, and Casten were sitting in our family room off the kitchen watching TV.

Jameson glared offensively at their mess on the coffee table of beer and a pizza box. "Don't you guys have homes to go to?"

I understood his annoyance considering what was going on, but I was also glad to see everyone. I didn't want to think about cancer. I just wanted to enjoy the moment.

"I don't question what my penis likes," Willie told Tommy, who was staring at the television like he was half asleep. "It just does what it wants. *And* she had asthma. It's a huge ego boost in bed."

It was then Casten noticed us. He had Gray on his lap, sound asleep and Hayden was on the floor, sleeping as well.

"Hey." Casten put his arm around me when I sat next to him, careful not to wake Gray. "You okay?"

If anyone could sense when something was wrong with me, it was Casten. We had always been close and aside from Jameson, no one could read me better than him, but I certainly wasn't ready to tell anyone so I carefully replied with, "Yeah, just tired."

"Where were you all day?" Rosa asked.

Jameson's eyes darted to mine, and then Rosa, his expression impassive. "None of your business."

"Don't be so mean." Smiling at him, Jameson dropped his stare to Rosa's shirt, squinting as he read the logo across the chest.

"Is that my fucking shirt?"

Rosa glanced down at his shirt, the one she stole from him. "No, I have one like it." And then she casually took a drink of her beer.

"Why exactly are you guys here?" Jameson took a seat next to me on the L-shaped couch surrounding our flat screen television on the wall.

"I was here first," Rosa noted. "I was vacuuming, and then all these assholes showed up."

I doubt Rosa was vacuuming, but stranger things had happened.

"Hey." Willie looked at Tommy. "Do you have any more of those ja-lap-ano chips?"

Tommy snorted, shaking his head as though he was thoroughly disappointed in him. "You mean the jalapeno ones?"

Casten snorted. "The J is a silent H, Willie. You're saying it wrong."

"Like Hal-a-peeno. That's how you say it," Tommy told him. "And no, I ate them. I love those delicious bastards."

It wasn't unusual to have so many people at our house. I actually enjoyed it. Having everyone nearby, sitting around casually, just existing with each other like it was the most natural thing, it was what I needed. My family.

I would never admit it to their faces, but our family wouldn't be complete without Tommy, Willie and Rosa. It just wouldn't. They have become as much a part of us as our own flesh and blood.

Jameson nodded to Tommy and Willie, still talking about what I assumed was Willie's date the other night. "Why are you two here?" he asked shrewdly.

They both looked at one another and then said, "Ran out of beer."

At least they were honest.

Rolling his eyes, Jameson leaned his weight into me, his warmth causing me to nearly sigh outwardly. And then I thought, I had breast cancer.

What if I don't get this very much longer?

This. All of it from the house full of family to the feeling of his heat as he leans against me? Jameson must have noticed my shocking reality sinking in, or the war in my head when he asked, "Are you tired, honey?"

He knew I couldn't sleep, but that was his way of asking if I wanted to go upstairs.

Did I? Would he want to talk? Could I handle that?

I gave him a nod as Tommy and Willie continued their debate across from us. "Sure. Are you?"

He leaned in closer, his breath blowing over my cheek as he spoke. "I'm gonna go upstairs." And then he reached for my hand, his silent invitation for me to follow.

The nice thing about our house was we could have fifty people inside, but our bedroom was our own private sanctuary.

After kissing the top of Gray's head, I took Jameson's hand and glanced at Casten. "Don't set anything on fire."

He grinned, running his hands through his nearly one-year-old daughter's hair, and it reminded me of him as a child, only it made my heart ache. Would I be around to see her grow or would I be cheated out of getting to witness her life like my parents were?

Why did cancer even exist?

I wanted to look at the bright and shiny positive side, but it was so hard because what if there wasn't a bright shiny side?

As I looked at my husband, watching him undress and slipping into bed, I thought back to the first time I ever slept in a bed with him. Not just anytime, the first time his arms snaked around my waist and pulled me in.

It was our summer, and we were in Cottage Grove at a hotel where we slept in our clothes. What always stayed with me was the way he pulled me in, and I forgot about everything else. At the time, I wasn't in love with him, but he always had that way about him. A simple look, a hug, a gentle pull of my body and I didn't have to think anymore.

I guessed, in some ways, I was still looking for that.

Laughing at the memory of him waking up in the morning handcuffed to the bed, my laugh sparked his smile. "What?"

Removing my shirt, I slipped his T-shirt over my shoulders and crawled into our bed. "I was thinking back to that time in Cottage Grove when Spencer handcuffed us to the bed."

His eyes dropped from mine to the bed as he pulled back the blankets to get in. "What made you think about that?"

"I was just... thinking about how anytime something was bothering me, it was never that bad as long as I had you there with me." I turned my body to face him when he didn't speak, not surprised by the pained expression he wore.

His lips pursed as he nodded once and hung his head. "I'm with you." His voice shook around the words, pushed out in a heavy breath from deep within. "I *won't* give up until the engine lets go and then, we rebuild. Whatever the cost, we *fucking* rebuild."

I smiled as a tear slid down my cheek. He always knew exactly what to say to make me feel better and how to say it.

CHAPTER FOUR — JAMESON

Brake Duct — A tube that takes air from the front or side of a car and directs it to the brakes in order to cool them.

MAY 2028

WHY HER?

I asked myself that a lot lately. Hadn't she been through enough? There were times I wondered if there was a god because how could he fucking do this to her?

How could he possibly take her from me?

And then I would think, fuck, why was I thinking of myself? This wasn't just about me.

I went through thousands of thoughts over the next five months and focused on one.

The night she broke down, falling into my chest as she sobbed, "Why us?" was the night it hit me the hardest.

Not why me. I understood why she said it that way because it was never her, or me, it was us. Together.

A feeling had started in my gut rising daily until I couldn't avoid it any longer. I didn't want the uneasiness anymore.

Cancer could potentially take my wife from me.

We had no other options. Surgery used to be our last option but it had become our only option.

This wasn't happening. It couldn't be. How could someone possibly take her from me?

It was late when I arrived home from the shop. We were set to leave for Lawrenceburg the following morning, and I had been trying to get the cars ready with the boys. I took a nasty hit a few nights earlier in Charlotte, and it did a number on my car and body. I had bruises all over me from that wreck.

By the time I walked through the bedroom door, Sway was laying buck-ass naked on the bed, waiting for me. I'll admit, it'd been a little while since we had sex and mostly because she was sick and I was afraid of hurting her.

Shutting the door and locking it, I gave her a wink. "Looks like pit lanes open," I teased.

Smiling, she raised her legs up and crossed them giving me a nice view between her legs. "Make love to me," she begged, blinking slowly as she watched me undress and crawl into bed with her. "That's all I want right now."

With a low groan, I pulled her face to mine, pressing my lips to hers. "I'll never deny you anything you want." There was truth in that statement, one she knew very well.

I wanted to be able to let go. I wanted to take her the way I wanted without restraints, but I couldn't.

Our lovemaking was different that night. Sway and I, we were good at the dirty talking and everything but there was a handful of occasions where nothing was said, only looks exchanged, and love bled between two people, a husband and a wife coming together.

Open mouths, tongues, hands, hips meeting with a desire that couldn't be broken, twisting to get closer, it was a blur, but I wouldn't have had it any other way.

My palm found her jaw, my thumb lazily brushing over her lip as I tilted her face to mine, parting my lips over hers.

Sway once told me, and I believed it, life was never perfect. No matter how hard you fucking tried, even the strongest crumbled and fell to their knees, myself included. Legends fell, heroes became normal fucking people and like that moment, with her, I was normal. I wasn't anything but Sway Riley's husband and fucking honored to be. That—right then—the tie that held us together as I moved inside of her was quite possibly the only thing holding us together.

It was different as I moved languidly against her, hips meeting hers with slow ardent movements I knew she needed. I'd like to say my kisses were different, slow, deep, and warm, wanting to show her how much I loved her through them.

Savoring the warmth spreading throughout me, I bent down to kiss her forehead, rocking myself into her as my control slipped and my orgasm threatened.

When I leaned back to look at her, her features held an emotion I couldn't decipher, or maybe she didn't want me to. All I know was it was something like love, but more devotion than anything.

My mouth moved from hers, spreading kisses over her jaw and against her neck. Unnerved by the tears forming in my eyes, I buried my head in her neck, hiding away from her. It was then her tears mixed with mine, rolling over her cheeks.

"Sway honey." My low timbre drew her attention, my nose brushing over her jaw.

Turning to look at me, I took a sharp intake of breath. Without saying the words, her face told me everything. She was scared of what the next month would bring for her, for us.

"I'm sorry," I mumbled, my hands trembling as they caressed her. "I'm sorry.... I'm *so* fucking sorry I can't make this go away," I cried against her shoulder, still moving inside her.

She grabbed my face between her hands. "I'm not asking you to. I just want you right now. Only you."

I couldn't look away from her right then. Leaning forward, my lips pressed to her neck.

Moaning, she arched against me, her legs wrapping tightly around my waist as she drew me deeper inside, biting softly down on my shoulder.

The release and relief were intense, our bodies melting into one another.

"Sway," I whispered, lips urgent against hers. "Fuck... you feel so good." I threw myself into my movements, chasing my orgasm I couldn't hold back any longer. My entire body jerked in time with my release, my head buried in her shoulder as she held my body tightly against hers.

I tried to be careful, but my body collapsed against hers, my breath hot and rapid on her neck. As she stroked my back tenderly, my own breathing and heart rate returned to a normal pace and reality hit me as I laid my cheek against her breast.

Exhaling heavily, I slid to one side bringing her to my chest.

Lying there quietly staring at each other, listening to the sounds outside our open window, she touched my face; her palm pressed to my cheek. "Don't be scared, Jameson."

How could she say that to me? Did she not realize what it meant if I lost her? Did she not realize there was no me without her?

I believed that without a doubt. It was the end of both of us.

Sway was my prayer, my blessing and sometimes curse. Nothing mattered but her. Maybe that was slightly a lie. Racing fucking mattered, but she was part of that. In many ways, she would *always* hold the checkered flag in our life without even knowing. My race and where I finished depended on her.

The expression I saw on her face took my breath away. I couldn't think. I couldn't speak. I just stared, transfixed looking into her eyes. Mesmerized by the depth of her passion for us I saw there.

I COULDN'T SLEEP that night, so I grabbed a case of beer and headed across the street to our lake. I lounged in a chair, my phone connected to speakers beside me playing on shuffle everything from Eric Church to Zac Brown Band.

"Are you okay?" Twisting my head, I noticed Arie standing on the dock.

Squeezing my burning eyes shut, I shook my head. "I'm fine."

I once asked myself would racing always be enough, would I eventually say when and give it all up?

Maybe without warning, your life, your body or maybe your mind had a way of saying it for you. This was me, again, saying when. *Give me my fucking wife and make her healthy.* I'd give up everything else for that.

Arie was quiet for a moment and then noticed my appearance. There was no doubt everyone knew something was wrong. We couldn't hide any longer, but I also couldn't tell Arie without Sway.

"Mom's sick... isn't she?"

Giving the lake a contemplative stare, I couldn't say the words to her because, in reality, I couldn't say them myself. Nodding was my only answer.

It wasn't that I couldn't tell her right then; I was honestly afraid if I said the words, I'd break down in front of her, and I was holding so strongly to my courage that I didn't want to break in front of my daughter. But I couldn't help it; the tears fell regardless of the tough exterior I'd been holding onto.

Arie stood for a moment and then began to leave. I didn't want her to leave and handed her a beer. "Stay?"

Our eyes caught in the night. Hers lit by the lanterns around us, misty-eyed and looking for comfort too. "Okay."

Taking a seat next to me, we sat in silence drinking and watching the lake until the song "Sweet Annie" finished, I looked over at her.

God, she reminded me so much of Sway at her age. Not in her looks—no that was all me— but in the way she carried herself and how she knew if someone needed to talk or just to sit side-by-side and stare at the lake. That was all Sway. She always knew what someone needed, most of the time even before they did.

Sitting, staring at our daughter, all I could think about was how grateful I was for the family Sway had given me. It wasn't just about the three amazing kids we raised. It was about the home and sense of security she always provided for all of us in a lifestyle full of unknowns. Sway was our foundation, and I would be thankful every damn day that one night in Charlotte I finally had the courage to ask her to stay.

Looking back at Arie, I could see the tension in her posture. She was battling her own demons and even though I told myself I wouldn't interfere with her life, she was my little girl and when she was hurting, so was I.

"I love you. You know that, right?" All my children knew I loved them, even Casten knew, but I needed to say it aloud as a way of telling her I was there for her no matter what.

Arie turned to me, giving me a soft smile that didn't reach her eyes. "Yeah, Dad, I know. I love you, too."

"I know we haven't always agreed on some of the choices you've made in life, but I hope you know that your mom and I, we're really proud of the woman you've grown to be."

It was true. Arie had made some bad decisions when she was young, usually regarding the opposite sex, but she had grown to be a smart and confident woman with a good head on her shoulders.

Staring at the lake, I hoped it gave some sort of answers to all of life's questions in the rippling water.

"Thanks," she finally said, her gaze slipping to her hands and the ring on her finger. "That means a lot to me."

"So what are you doing here anyway?" I asked, wondering why she showed up in Mooresville of all places tonight. "Shouldn't you be with your husband in Charlotte?" As soon as I asked the question, I could see that it was the wrong question to ask by the way her body went from calm to rigid. Immediately her back straightened, and her stare moved away from me back to the lake. Almost like she was trying to hide some sort of emotion from me. That I was used to. Arie had always been my secretive child. In order to get anything out of her, you had to pry, and if you pried too much, you'd get nothing. It was a thin line to balance.

"I was, but he was hanging out drinking with Jacob and Brody in the pits, so I decided to come home for the night." My instincts told me there was more to the story, but I could tell it wasn't something she wanted to talk about, so I let it go.

I knew the feeling of not wanting to open up just yet.

WHEN I WAS back in the house, I stumbled around the room from having a case of beer in me.

Down on my knees next to the bed, I watched her sleeping that night.

Staring at her, I brushed a stray hair that had fallen over her forehead. I tried to be careful because I didn't want to wake her and lose the moment to just be beside her. To just sit and admire this beautiful and remarkable woman who deserved to sleep without worries or cares. I prayed that at least in her sleep, Sway could dream of happier times without the fear of what the next month would bring us. Without the fear of the unknown. I prayed I would carry the burden alone, at least until morning.

Naturally, sitting and watching someone else sleep gave me plenty of time to start questioning all of my life choices. The main one being why hadn't I spent more time at home with my family, with Sway?

Why had I put racing before her for so many years?

It was a stupid question because the thing was, it was hard to rationalize giving up or cutting back on racing because this was a lifestyle Sway wanted as much as I did. If by chance we were rained out at night, she was just as upset as me.

If we broke something on the car or had a bad finish, I saw the look on her face. Disappointment. She was just as competitive as I was.

It was crazy to think she would want me to give up. No, I was sure it was just the opposite. I was convinced she would have fought me every step of the way had I told her I wanted to stop racing to be home more.

We made our life work. I knew that. But I also knew our life worked because of her. Without her, it all fell to shit.

CHAPTER FIVE —SWAY

Casing – The tire body beneath the tread and sidewalls.

JUNE 2028

I TOLD MYSELF when my father died of brain cancer and kept it from me, I would never keep something like this from my children. Unfortunately, I understood why Charlie kept it from me. And I totally understood *why* my mother did. Jack was the same age I was when my mother died, and I didn't think he could comprehend what that meant.

Maybe that was why she didn't tell me. Had she known I wouldn't have understood?

Probably. My mother was a smart woman. I'd like to think I was a little bit like her, if not just in looks.

"Should we tell them?" I asked Jameson as we lay in bed.

No way did I want to start today out like this, telling my family I had cancer, but in some ways I wanted to get it over with and move on.

"That's up to you, honey. They should know. Arie knows you're sick."

He was right. He always had a way of being my reasoning. I needed to tell them.

The time came to tell them. I couldn't keep it from them any longer, and I didn't want to.

It happened before we left for Kokomo Speedway. Arie watched me closely that afternoon and I knew it was coming.

"I know something's going on," she noted, leveling me with a serious stare. I'd seen the look a lot from her growing up. Mostly when she was calling me out on being a shitty mother or the time I forgot to feed her all day when she was four. It happened frequently when you had three kids and a crazy life. If they didn't say anything, how was I to know?

Straightening my posture, I looked her in the eye. I couldn't keep pretending any longer and honestly, I didn't want to. If anything, I wanted my daughter to know because I wanted her with me. "There is."

"You said you would never keep a secret from us," she reminded me.

I said that, didn't I?

"It's not that I'm keeping a secret." *Lie. You were.* "It's that I didn't know *how* to tell you kids." *And that's the honest to God truth.* "I always told myself I wouldn't keep anything from you kids, but it was harder to tell you than I realized it would be."

Her breath drew out long and slow as if to prepare herself. "What's wrong?"

Drawing in my own deep breath, I set the bag aside, unable to keep the tears at bay any longer. "I have breast cancer." I hated the way it sounded saying it out loud, as if it were a death sentence. "Stage two. My doctor found the lump when I went in for my yearly mammogram."

She blinked twice before asking, "Can you beat it?"

"It's still contained to the breast tissue." My emotions had gotten the better of me; my face clouded with unease. "So, the doctors have assured me that it's the best-case scenario... I'm hopeful."

Hopeful was right. It was all I could have been at that point.

"How is Dad taking this?"

Horribly. I remembered his face, the way the color drained and the distance in his eyes. Every detail of that morning came crashing back to me including his temper tantrum in the doctor's office. "He was with me when I found out and you know him, he's internalizing a lot."

And sometimes physically displaying his anger.

"How long has this been going on?"

"We found out in December, right before Christmas, and tried some herbal remedies. They didn't work so we went to see a specialist in Charlotte two months ago."

"What did dad say about all this?"

I thought back to everything he'd said to me over the last few months and though all of it was encouraging, that first night stood out. "He said he's in it with me. He said we don't give up until the engine lets go." My smile overtook me. "And then we rebuild. Whatever the cost, we rebuild."

Arie's tears fell hopelessly down her face as she chuckled at her dad's words. "Of course he said that." There was a moment where she remained quiet and then looked at me. "What are they going to do?"

Nonchalantly I replied with, "Cut the funbags off and give me new upgraded ones." I admitted, getting perky funbags was actually something I wanted. My sweet, bratty children had sucked the life right out of them. They needed some inflation for sure.

"Do you have to have radiation and chemo?"

"No. They think they can get it because it hasn't spread to the lymph nodes. I had yearly mammograms, so it was an early detection."

"Then why have you been losing so much weight and disappearing right before our eyes? Everyone's worried about you, Mom."

"Arie, it's just the stress and the not knowing that's weighing heavily on me," I told her, hoping she understood I *never* wanted to keep this from her. "I promise that I've told you everything now, and that's also been part of the problem, keeping it from you kids and the family has been harder on me than you can ever imagine. My mom died of breast cancer, and I didn't even know she had it until she died. I told myself I would tell you kids but when I found out... I couldn't do it."

She hugged me immediately, and I was on the verge of losing it all together. Arie wasn't a hugger, much like her father, but when she did hug you, it was one you knew meant something, delivered perfectly timed and for a reason.

Jameson came in, assessing our embrace and tears, pushing his hat up with his left hand, he knew something was up. "What's wrong?"

Brushing my tears away with the sleeve of her sweatshirt, I watched Jameson carefully. "I told Arie."

Sighing with what seemed like relief at first, his eyes watered as though it hit him again, another wave of uncertainty.

"We gotta go." He motioned toward the door with a nod. "Plane's waiting."

AFTER THAT WEEKEND in Kokomo Speedway, and telling our entire family, it seemed I constantly remembered things he'd said to me over the years when I found a note Jameson had written to me not long after his crash in Knoxville where Jimi died.

After we told the kids, and the rest of the family, it seemed they were intent on making sure we knew we had their support. Which I appreciated but a sense of fear came with that too because I didn't want to worry anyone. They wouldn't stop fussing over me, and I found myself in our closet a lot hiding out.

It was during those times that I was able to sit and think, where I was constantly remembering things Jameson had said to me over the years. And then I found a note he'd written me not long after his accident in Knoxville where Jimi died and Jameson was injured badly.

Sitting back against a pile of shoes I read a note. The one he wrote while I was going through my porn star days. I tried so hard to find the connection I thought we lost that I had missed it all along. Jameson reminded me then, and even now.

Sway,

So many times over the last few months I've wanted

to ease your pain tell you that everything was going to be all right, but I didn't know if it would. I also knew that

it wouldn't change anything if I didn't feel it.

Watching you sleep now, I'm reminded of what I

haven't considered over that time and what I nearly lost.

You.

I know I've been distant and unlike the man you

grew to love surrounded by one dream and one lifestyle.

Taught to feel you, to feel me, and to feel us once again

as one, was like being able to breathe again

Our love was cultivated in the shadows and at a time

that we least expected it. It shines through the darkest

of moments, never fading, always triumphing over the

heartache we have suffered.

You are the light that pulls the boy in me from

anonymity and gives me a true purpose in a life of

vulnerability and frustration. I wonder, looking at you in the purest form if I could have been a better husband or

father I wonder if you know how much I love you. I think

the world of you

without you, all the trophies and titles in the world mean

nothing In the blinding spotlight my life has created it's

you who brings me back

Our life is measured in moments Moments that test us,

challenge us and moments that make us fall to our fucking

knees begging and pleading for all we're worth for just one

more moment.

With you, I don't want to ever be out of moments I

want to feel my heated cheek against your skin as the

world stay is spoken I want to watch your eyes light up

when I vow forever. I want to watch you hold three

precious angels I want to laugh with you, cry with you, and

be one with you. Forever one heart and one soul.

I'll never let you go

You are where my heart belongs

Jameson

When I finished, I burst into tears, clutching the letter to my chest, much like I did that damn photograph I had taken from the magazine. Which, by the way, was inside the same box with the letter, wrinkled edges, and everything. I remembered sitting on that bathroom floor and tearing it from the magazine.

Gasping, I gently took the worn paper in my hand. It seemed so crazy to think it was from six years earlier when it felt like yesterday.

CHAPTER SIX —JAMESON

Harness – The safety belt system worn by a driver.

"**WHAT ARE YOU** *doing?"*

"You said you needed to be rescued. Are you coming or not?"
Sway asked breathlessly. *"The food is getting cold."*

"You brought food?"

"Well, yeah. I was hungry."

"I haven't climbed out my window in years," I admitted,
climbing out nonetheless. After falling about five feet, I landed on
my ass with Sway standing over me laughing.

"Smooth, Riley. Real smooth,"

I glared at her as she brushed grass and dirt from my tux. *"I
should have changed."*

Sway glanced in my direction.

"Nah, you look good." She winked. *"Keep it on."*

That was when I finally looked at Sway's appearance. While
she looked beautiful as always, I had to laugh at her attire. She had
on a black tutu over her jeans. *"What's with the tutu?"*

"It's prom, isn't it?" Her brow furrowed like I was stupid for
asking. *"This is my dress."*

I shook my head. It fit her personality perfectly. She wasn't the type of girl to go for the gown. She was simplicity.

A few minutes later, we were sitting inside Emma's tree house eating Chinese food. I could always count on Sway to bail me out of situations. I laughed to myself at the thought of Chelsea looking for me at the dance, but I was almost certain she'd find someone to dance with. There were times where I felt bad for the way I treated Chelsea, but I was also well aware of the guys she flirted with and did God knows what with when I was out of town. I wasn't stupid. We'd used each other.

In the distance, we watched as Tommy picked up Emma for the dance. They were going as friends, but that didn't stop me from threatening to cut off his balls if he tried anything.

Mom fussed endlessly over her dress while we laughed. I knew damn well I'd catch hell from mom over this but, like always, I didn't care.

As I took a bite of my egg roll, I noticed Sway gazing at Mom and Emma talking.

Unbuttoning the top buttons of my shirt, I attempted to get more comfortable.

"Do you miss her?" I asked softly, leaning into her shoulder.

"Miss who?" I knew she knew who I was referring to but was stalling. She fidgeted with the ruffles on her tutu.

"Your mom?"

Sway was silent for a long moment eating her noodles before sighing and leaning back on the wooden floor of the tree house. Setting down my food, I lay next to her.

"I miss her," she mused, nodding once. "I don't remember much about her. I wish I did... I feel like I constantly forget memories that I wish I wouldn't."

"What do you remember?"

We had talked about Rachel every now and then, but it wasn't a typical conversation. Sway was a happy-go-lucky type of girl, and that was what I loved about her. It was refreshing. She'd rather have good memories than bad, and she'd rather laugh than cry.

"I still remember what she smelled like." I watched her face closely as a tear slid down her cheek. "Bananas and coconut. It was a perfume she had I assume, but I'll never forget it."

"I'm sorry." I reached for her hand taking it in mine, intertwining our fingers together. "I shouldn't have asked."

"No." She wiped tears away. "I miss her. It's okay to talk about it. With you, I can talk about it."

"Come here." I pulled her into my arms trying to comfort her in any way I could.

Though I had an idea of the pain, I had no idea how much living without her mom hurt her. Other than my Uncle Lane dying when I was nine, we hadn't lost anyone in our family. My grandparents were still alive and, aside from my mom's parents who had died in a car accident on New Year's Eve when she was seven, I'd never had to deal with this kind of loss.

My mom did, and I think that was why she and Sway got along so well. She understood what Sway was going through.

"Thanks for not going to the dance," she told me after a good ten minutes of silence.

"No problem." I chuckled against her shoulder. "Do you know what would make this night fun?"

"I could use some entertainment." She turned in my arms. "What did you have in mind?"

"Refilling Emma's lotions with glue again and cutting holes in Spencer's underwear." I stood to help her up. *"Our usual madness."*

"Sounds like fun."

Laughing at the memory, I smiled when Sway came downstairs that night. We'd just gotten back from Knoxville Speedway the night before and set to leave a few days later for Sauk Rapids, but I was taking Sway on a date. Just the two of us.

Setting her small black bag on the table, she eyed me carefully. It kind of scared me. She looked... upset?

"What?"

"I want to have sex on the hood of your car. I got dressed up in a dress, shaved my legs. I want to be wooed like we used to."

Wooed? Immediately I thought of Key West when we had sex in an alley. So did my dick.

"Okay." I stood before her, my body fully in line with hers. "Let's do it. Right now. Car's in the garage."

"I mean..." And then I realized quickly where this was going and shook my head. "...I mean your Mustang," she stuttered out, biting down on her lower lip.

The color drained from my face. No one touched that car. Hell, I only drove it a couple times a year, and it wasn't even worth it because I spent the entire time making sure nothing touched it. This 1969 Shelby Mustang GT500 was a rare original. I hadn't touched anything on it, still had almost everything original aside from a custom paint job. I bought it when I was sixteen. A few speeding tickets later, I sold it to my dad, and then once I signed with a NASCAR team, I bought it back from him.

"Sway... anything but that," I finally said, feeling my face heat now. I knew she was going to cry.

"Fine," she huffed. "Whatever. Just take me out then." Reaching for her bag, we headed to the garage to my Aston Martin, the car I thought she'd been talking about. Hell, I didn't even keep the Mustang here at the house because of my irresponsible shithead of a son.

Once we were in the car and on our way to the restaurant, Sway wouldn't even look at me. She was pissed, and she was going to make sure I knew it.

"Look, honey." I placed my hand on her thigh. "You know I love you, and I would do anything for you, but this is where I have to draw the line." It was true, I would do *anything* to make my wife happy, but having sex on the hood of my Mustang was the one thing I just couldn't do.

"It's fine," she clipped, pushing my hand off her thigh. "I'm just glad to know where I stand with you."

The hell? "What's that supposed to mean?"

Turning to me, a look of distaste crossed her face. "What I mean is I'm glad I know where I stand. Your love for your car rates higher than your love for me. It's okay. I understand. I'm only your wife after all. The woman who birthed your three children and all."

She was good, I'd give her that, but there was no way I was going to back down on this. Not a fucking chance.

When we finally pulled into the restaurant, Sway still wouldn't talk to me and to be honest, it was starting to fucking piss me off.

Once we were seated and had ordered our food, I decided that two could play at this game.

"You know, I could say the same to you," I told her, taking a drink of my beer.

Sway finally looked up from her phone that she had been using to distract herself from talking to me. "Oh yeah? How do you figure?"

Leaning forward, I placed my elbows on the table locking my hands together as I stared directly into her eyes. "Well, by the way you're behaving, you're basically telling me that having sex on the Mustang is more important to you than *my* feelings."

Sitting back in my chair, never losing eye contact, I felt pretty good about the fact that I had turned this around on her when she just burst out laughing. Fucking laughing.

"What the hell is so funny?"

"You. *You're* what's so funny." Slowly, she took a drink of her own beer raising it to her lips and then setting it softly down on the table before eyeing me carefully. "Seriously, Jameson? You expect me to believe your precious feelings are hurt because I asked you to fuck me on the hood of your precious Mustang. Give me a break. That's laughable."

I didn't like where this was going.

"I have feelings, you know. I'm not just some sex machine you can tell to fuck you anywhere you want." It was a lie and she fucking knew it. Usually, she mentioned the word sex and my pants were coming off. So naturally, my reply made her laugh harder. I had to admit it was a stupid statement, but she was pushing my buttons.

After like five fucking minutes, Sway finally calmed down and wiped the tears from her laughter off her cheeks. She took a deep breath settling back into her chair.

"Stop laughing at me," I grumbled, sulking in my defeat.

"I know how much you love that car. I really do, but with everything going on and the surgery coming up I just thought maybe we could do something different, reckless even like we used to when we were younger," she said, her eyes holding emotions I didn't know were there. "We had so much fun back then, and I just thought it would be incredibly hot to have my dirty heathen fuck his pit lizard on a car almost as sexy as he is... that's all."

She had me there.

Raising my eyes from hers, I searched the restaurant. "Where's that damn waitress so we can get the check?"

"Really?" She watched me with wide-eyed excitement.

"Yeah, really." I nodded to the door. "Now let's go before I change my mind."

I'd never seen Sway move so fast in heels. The way she squealed as she jumped out of her chair and grabbed my hand to pull me outside was fucking adorable. I couldn't help laughing at her eagerness, but also wanting to kick myself for ever thinking I *wouldn't* give her what she wanted. Sway was more important than anything else in this life and if it took fucking her on the hood of my Mustang to prove it to her, then that was exactly what I was going to do.

"**WHERE THE HELL** are we going? Are we even in Mooresville still?"

"Close your eyes. I don't want anyone knowing where this is in case you somehow tell Casten."

Sighing, she closed her eyes. "I won't tell him."

"Uh-huh."

And then she stared at me as we pulled up to the building, completely ignoring my request for her not to look. "You're being dramatic."

She had no idea. I kept this car in a warehouse I owned, with a security code only I knew.

I had to keep the car someplace safe since my youngest son took it upon himself to destroy my vehicles. He'd caught not two, but three of my cars on fire and managed to land one in our pool.

The warehouse was in an industrial park outside Mooresville with about three other buildings and a body shop across the street.

Once inside, I flipped on the light and leaned into the wall as Sway walked past me to the car.

"Fuck me, Jameson," she moaned. "I need you inside of me, now."

I certainly wasn't going to deny her, but fuck, seeing her beg for a little was hot.

"What do you mean, inside you?" I grinned. Fuck yeah, I was gonna make her beg a little. I was about to have sex with her on a car worth roughly a million dollars. It would require some convincing.

"What I mean is"—she stepped out of her dress leaving it a mess on the floor in front of me and placed her hands carefully on the hood of the car, glancing back at me over her shoulder—"I need to be align bored. And if you're not willing to do it, well then..." Her right hand made a lazy path of her hips and between her legs. "...maybe I'll just have to do it myself, and you can watch me. But I sure would like your camshaft doing the work."

Okay, well as hot as that would be to see her getting herself off, I didn't like my wife satisfying her need herself. It was my job.

But I played it cool. I wouldn't be me if I didn't. "I don't know," I said, shaking my head.

"What you mean is you don't know if you can handle it, right?"

Sway sprawled herself out on the hood, much like the night I fucked her on the hood of my race car and sprint car a few years back.

I wanted to tease her a little, why not, right?

Stepping toward her, I took my time removing my shirt and then unbuttoned my pants but left them open in the front. When I reached her, I let my pants slide down and stepped out of them.

Shaking her hips, she ground herself back against my erection when I stepped forward. I growled gutturally as the angle set my already raw nerves ablaze.

Spreading her legs apart a little more, I positioned myself at her entrance and then pushed forward, not waiting. "You were saying something about not being able to handle it?"

"Nothing. I was saying nothing!" She screamed, her voice shaking with each hard thrust I delivered. Spreading my legs out a little further, I gained the leverage needed and leaned in to rest my weight against her back, pressing her body into the cool metal hood.

"Is this what you wanted, honey?" I hissed between thrusts. "Do you like being fucked on the hood of a car?"

She moaned in approval, saying nothing in reply, her eyes drifting closed as my left hand remained latched tightly to her hips.

"Yes," she moaned. "I needed this so badly." She cried out once more as I fisted my hand in her hair. Her pleasure, so stunning, was almost too much to watch, but I did. I couldn't tear my eyes away from it even if I wanted to.

Just when she thought this would be a standard "let's get this done because you might scratch the paint," I showed her a different side and pushed the remote to the stereo hooked up to my phone. "Closer" by Nine Inch Nails blared through the warehouse as I twisted her hair around my hand and yanked backward.

"Now...." Her head snapped back, not hard, but enough I had her attention as I bit down on the nape of her neck. "I hope you're ready for some press forging."

The breath expelled from her lungs in a gasp, and she giggled. "Hot *fucking* damn."

Turning her around so I could see all of her, I wanted to climb up there with her, much like the night on the hood of my race car, but with the possibility of denting the hood, I refrained.

She noticed my hesitation to get up there with her and raised an eyebrow. "Really, Jameson?"

So I got on the hood. If I was going to woo her, I had to take one for the team.

Settling between her legs, my right hand reached for her left knee to draw it up my hip. "How about this?" My hips pushed forward, giving her one hard thrust.

The thrust scooted her further up the hood, her head falling back against the metal with a thump.

There was no more talking after that. Once I hooked my hand on the hood, I gave her what she needed. She wanted this hard and fast, and fuck, I wanted that too.

"I love you," I told her, my voice husky.

She moaned against me. "Thank you, for this." Eagerly, she kissed my shoulder and then my neck. "I love you so much." With each thrust inside her, she fell apart in my hands; her body bare for me to take what I wanted, her beauty as blinding as the sun.

Gasping, her eyes rolled back as I pulled her leg up around my waist higher. "I fucking love you so much."

Our movements turned frantic. Arms, hands and legs flailing around, my knees aching as I searched for angles and our need. As we rocked against each other, the hood creaked with each thrust. Clutching at me, her nails dug into my skin, slipping over my shoulders, moaning and tossing her head back and forth against the hood.

Sway moaned and with one last thrust, I was done, just as the song was coming to an end. The relief and euphoria poured through me in waves as an animalistic growl rang throughout the warehouse, echoing off the walls.

Not sure how much time went by, but eventually we released each other. When I looked at Sway, her eyes were closed, her hands running through my hair.

"Is that what you wanted?" I murmured eventually.

"Exactly what I wanted." She chuckled.

I tried like hell to enjoy that moment with her afterward, but I couldn't help myself and my poor car.

"We can get up. It's not like I need a post-race victory lap or anything."

"Oh, thank fuck." I jumped off the hood and hauled her off it too, inspecting every inch for damage.

"Oops, there's a scratch," Sway noted, pointing to the center of the hood.

My eyes snapped to where she was pointing.

There wasn't one.

CHAPTER SEVEN — JAMESON

Reverse Cooling – A method of routing engine coolant to reduce differences in temperature between different parts of the head in the block.

TOMMY SCRATCHED THE side of his head, pantless, and rolled onto his stomach on the concrete. It was then he noticed he didn't have any pants on. "Have you seen my pants?"

"Try Casten's front yard," Sway told him looking away from his morning wood as he stood. "That's where I saw them last."

Shaking my head, Sway and I walked back inside the house only to find a goat eating out of our fridge. It was no surprise—we had a party last night. It didn't start out as a party. It never did but then someone shows up to drink or hang out because no one ever hung out at their own fucking house, and before we knew it, the sun was coming up and usually Tommy, Willie or Dave were passed out in our backyard.

"What *is* that?" Sway asked when we were in the kitchen.

I glared at the furry animal in my kitchen. "A fucking goat."

The damn thing turned around, took one look at Sway and ran up to her rubbing against her like a dog in heat.

Sway looked as if she was ready to nurse the goddamn thing and she hugged it to her side. "Can we keep him? He's *so* cute."

"No way." I picked up my phone. I knew without a doubt Aiden was behind it and that grass-loving motherfucker was going to pay.

I mean, a fucking goat in my house?

"There's a goat eating lettuce out of my fridge," I told Aiden when he picked up the phone. "You better run, asshole."

All I heard was laughter when I ended the call as Casten came walking through the door with Gray on his shoulders eating what looked to be a chocolate donut. "Where'd the donkey come from?" he asked, smiling.

"Fucking Aiden."

When I turned back around to talk to Sway about what to do with the damn goat, I found her sitting on the floor with it between her legs licking her face. I almost vomited. Straight up bile rising up into my throat. I could taste it.

I started to walk toward them so I could drag the disgusting animal outside and demand, from a distance, that Sway head upstairs and wash the goat slobber off her face. The thought of goat's saliva on my skin made me want to run, run far away and then scrub my skin raw.

When I was close enough to grab the goat by the neck, it turned and screamed at me while lunging my way. Full on, high-pitched, teenage-girl screamed. Who knew a goat could make that noise? But it could.

"The fuck!" I jumped back, practically on the table, only to have Gray belly laugh at me. Apparently, she thought it was the funniest thing she'd ever seen. I wasn't sure if it was the goat screaming, or the fact that I was scared of it that entertained her more.

"Jameson!" Sway threw her arms around the goat and pulled it to her as if I was the one trying to kill it, not the other way around. "Stop, you're scaring it."

"*I'm* scaring it?" I stared at her in disbelief, scowling. "Are you fucking serious? It just tried to kill me!"

"Oh, it did not."

"It's really creepy looking," Casten noted, keeping his distance.

You would think my wife would side with me, but no, she was stroking this goat like it was her fourth child.

"I really do think we should keep him," Sway cooed, scratching its head. "I think he's just a baby. Look at how much he needs me?"

"No, Sway. No fucking way am I keeping that psychotic excuse for a goat." I shook my head adamantly and even pulled Gray away from it when she tried to feed it her donut. "No way."

"Well, what do you suggest we do with it then? Because I'm not just going to let you drop it off on some country road by itself to try and survive."

Gray, who seldom liked anyone, glared at me. "No, Papa." She stepped closer, only to have it lick the side of her face. That got her upset as she glared offensively at it. How dare it lick her, right? At least I knew she would eventually be on my side.

"Yeah, because dropping a goat off in a field full of grass would be cruel and unusual punishment." I slid off the table, still keeping my distance with Casten. "It's their natural habitat, Sway, a field with grass. It's like hitting the damn lottery for the stupid thing."

"No. We need to find it a home. Someplace it can feel safe and loved."

Was she serious? I was thinking she had to be joking, but when I looked at her face, the expression she shot my way told me otherwise. There was no way I was going to win this one.

"Okay. We'll find it a home," I eventually said and then whispered to Casten. "When we leave, put it in Spencer's backyard."

"Where it's safe and feels loved?" Sway asked, sticking her bottom lip out.

Sighing, I dropped my head, staring at the ground. Stupid fucking goat. "Yes, honey. A home where it feels safe and loved. Now can I please move the damn thing out of my kitchen?"

"Okay but if you're going to put it in the backyard, make sure it has plenty of shade and water."

Casten and I hauled the goat down the street to Spencer's house that morning before we needed to head to the shop. "I think you guys will still be at it when you're in your seventies."

All I could think was Aiden was gonna pay for this shit.

"Probably."

He laughed when the goat took a shit on my shoe.

I wasn't laughing one fucking bit.

"ARE YOU SURE you don't want to stay home this weekend?" I asked Sway when we were ready to leave.

"No. I'm coming with you," she said without question.

I should have known this wouldn't slow Sway down, and I also shouldn't have been surprised when she wanted to come to River Cities with us. In a way, I was banking on her wanting to be there because I had a surprise for her.

Finally, for once, or maybe it had all along, but this sport was giving her something back in return for everything it took from her. I would make sure of it. I would never stop trying to make this easy for her, and show her how much support she had in this place we called home.

From the dusty backstretch to the dry-slick wide sweeping turns, a dirt track was where I met her, and ultimately the place I fell in love. What better way to show her my heart still raced for her, but at the one place she could understand it, a dirt track.

"I will never stop trying to show you how much you mean to me," I told her before that race, knowing damn well she wouldn't know what I was talking about. "Now go sit in the stands."

She looked at me curiously. Sway was always in the pits with me. "Why?"

"Because sometimes it's fun to have you cheer me on from the stands like you did when we were kids."

She smiled, the gesture warming her cheeks. "That should be fun."

I was worried she'd see the paint schemes before we had a chance to show her on the track, but luckily, Arie and Alley had kept her from doing so by making sure she flew to the track with them, and me not letting her in the pits.

Hayden stood at the gate to the ticket booth waiting for Sway with the kids. "Come on already. I can't contain these little hoodlums forever."

Sway shook her head. "I think she needs some help."

Before she could get away, I pulled her in for a kiss. It was more than a standard good-luck kiss. This one had meaning for what I planned to do to her later tonight. Around us, the guys in the pit hooped and hollered, cheering us on.

"Wow," Sway breathed, shaking her head as she touched her fingers to her pink lips when I drew back.

I slapped her ass as she was walking away. "That's right."

Rager approached as I turned to walk back to my car, the faint rumblings of crews putting heat in the engines filling the air. "That was one hell of a good-luck kiss you got there, old man."

"Fuck off." I laughed, pushing past him and heading toward the pits.

Rager jogged to catch up to me keeping pace as we approached our cars. "So do you think she has any idea about her surprise?"

"Nah. The girls did a good job at keeping her distracted all day so she never really had a chance to see any of the cars."

"That's good." I turned to face him because it seemed like he had something more to say, but when I looked, his focus was elsewhere. Arie was walking by.

I'd known for a long time there was more to those two than what was being said, but it was a thought for another time. That night was about giving Sway something to smile about and nothing else.

Axel scratched the back of his head as he approached me. "Hey, Dad, so Arie and Casten mentioned doing a concert for Mom. What do you think?"

"Yeah, they may have said something about that."

"Are you going to?" he pressed, reaching for his helmet.

I thought about it for a while. I didn't want to, but this wasn't about me. It was about her. "I don't want to, but whatever you guys think she'd want, I'll do. The night needs to be about her."

For so long, our lives have been in the fast lane. Hell, we were in a different city every night sometimes so slowing down wasn't exactly easy for us. Cancer changed you emotionally. Everything I had been through or stressed about seemed insignificant.

For years, Sway and I had donated more money to breast cancer awareness than most charities we gave to. Never did I think I'd be

RACING ON THE EDGE

so thankful for the research they've done and what advances they've been able to make in the treatment of breast cancer.

Seeing how cancer ran in her family, I think it was always a fear of Sway's that eventually she'd be forced to deal with it. For a while, about four years ago, she had told me she wanted to get a mastectomy so she wouldn't have to deal with it.

I, unfortunately, talked her out of it. Couldn't even tell you why I did at the time. Selfish reasons maybe.

I felt like the biggest piece of shit now and was convinced she'd somehow blame me for this. But that wasn't Sway. Never would she blame someone else.

My decision to change the paint schemes for all the cars was easy. I did it without thinking. Even my sponsors were all for it once they discovered Sway had breast cancer. The hardest part of all of it was keeping Sway from seeing it because she was so thoroughly involved in every aspect of JAR Racing. Without a doubt, I wanted to make that night at River Cities Speedway special for her. Sure, I would have loved for it to happen at Grays Harbor but with the surgery scheduled soon, I didn't have time to wait until we were in Elma in September.

For that reason, I had the six JAR Racing sprint cars changed along with the Cup cars for five races. I even had a photograph taken of all of us standing in front of the cars. The cars were all black with a hot pink breast cancer symbol. The roll bars and helmets were hot pink too and made for an interesting look when you had them all on the track at the same time.

I couldn't see Sway's reaction to them when she first saw the cars on the track at the same time, but I had Alley record it for me.

I would have given anything to see her face during that four-wide salute because I knew how emotional it was for me right then. I'd be lying if I said I didn't get teary-eyed over it.

We were only one lap into the 40-lap feature when a car slid up the track in three and four. I chose the outside on the restart. When the green flag dropped, I ran the outside trying to find grip up there since there was nothing on the bottom. It was slick. My car was fucking fast all night, and soon I had a good lead on the entire field.

The race was caution filled, but I managed to get a good jump on each restart. Axel remained in second most of the race, and I constantly chose the inside line because I knew he was fast down there. Some would have said, give him the win. He's your son. Not me. If you wanted to win in this sport, you had to choose what was more important and chose quickly. No question, I wanted to win this race.

Believe it or not, I *never* let anyone win in my life, family or not. I would never want someone to let me win. I wanted to know I earned every race.

With some determination, Axel managed to grab the lead from me with four to go. I wasn't giving him more than a taste of it and snatched the lead back, giving myself a good two-second cushion to work with in those remaining laps.

On the final restart, Axel ran side-by-side with me but couldn't make the pass stick as we crossed the line.

Wanting to give Sway a sight she would appreciate, I did what they told me not to in the drivers meeting and did a couple of 360 turns before bringing the car down to the front stretch.

I had to take my time getting out of the car. Mostly because once again, the emotions, the unstableness clawing at me took over and I was left hanging on by a thread, ready to crumble at her feet and beg her to take this pain away. The thing was, it wasn't her pain to take away. She couldn't and shouldn't have to offer me anything. She was the one with cancer. I should be the strong one, the one she should be able to lean on.

Now look at me. A fucking mess.

Taking off the steering wheel, I set it on the dash and then pulled my belts loose. I was slow getting out, Sway watching my every move, but I gave her the sight she wanted.

I wasn't looking at her, at first, but I knew with how badly her body was shaking; she was struggling just as much as I was. Standing on the back of the car, I pounded my hands on the top wing of my car.

Slumping forward, my head rested on the wing as I prayed to my dad. *Please, Dad. If you have any control over the outcome of what she's going through, please don't let anyone take her from me,* I silently prayed. *Please, I'm fucking begging you here.*

Standing straight, I lifted my hand to the sky, holding my hand to him. *Thank you for everything you've taught me, including how to love her.*

When I jumped down, my stare found Sway as I removed my helmet. I didn't talk to the media; I didn't look at anyone but her. She knew what I was going to do before I even approached her, her smile so wide, tears running helplessly down reddened cheeks.

Stepping toward me, her arms wrapped around my shoulders as I pressed my lips to her. That kiss was significant, poignant in the bright lights around us as I held her against my body.

Normally, I wouldn't have kissed my wife like that in front of everyone, but right then, it didn't matter. My tongue swept over her lips, and she gladly opened hers wider, letting me kiss her the way I wanted. Groaning into her mouth, I tangled one gloved hand into her hair, securing her face to mine as I deepened the kiss.

It sent my stomach in a whirl, wanting more than a kiss, but not here. For the time being, she'd know where I intended this to go later.

Her posture weakened into me, her body giving in as I demanded a response. "Jameson," she gasped against my lips, surprised by my display in front of hundreds and hundreds of people watching us.

"I love you," I whispered, drawing back, brushing a gentle kiss across her forehead. "Don't you ever forget that." Unsure if she noticed, but a tired look of sadness passed over me when her glowing youthful happiness I usually saw had faded. It was clear she was sick. There was no denying it.

Kissing me once more, she stared at me. "I never could."

The announcer for the World of Outlaws sprint car tour approached me and smiled. "Jameson Riley, you won the dash and dominated that main. There seemed to be no question you would pull it off."

Laughing, I took the towel Sway handed me and wiped my face. "There's always a question when you got guys like Axel and Rager behind you. They're gassers. You earn it when you beat them."

The announcer's voice shook. He didn't want to ask, especially to someone who knocked him out once for taking a jab about my kid being handed his way in the sport. That was years ago; I was more mature, but I imagined he still thought twice before he asked me a question. "It seems like this is an emotional win for you. Tell us about this paint scheme you got going on and will it stay?"

"This is a very emotional win for us." I swallowed, hanging my head when my voice cracked. Looking up, tears fell from my eyes freely. Glancing at Sway, my chin shook. Damn it. I didn't want to cry in front of everyone. "This paint scheme is for her. My life. My *wife*...." Drawing in a deep, shaky breath, I blinked away the tears and ran my hand over my face. I didn't want to tell anyone about Sway's cancer, but then again, I couldn't keep this from everyone who supported us over the years. They deserved to know how hard she was fighting. "A few months ago my wife was diagnosed with breast cancer. This is for her. We're keeping this paint scheme on these cars for ten races and the Cup cars for five races."

Everyone, and I do mean everyone, in the bleachers gasped at the news; nothing was public until that moment. Even the announcer looked stunned, and he'd been literally around us all year.

Wrapping my arm around Sway, I squeezed her close. "She's strong, guys. If anyone can fight, it's Sway Riley." Our eyes locked, a tearful smile on both parts. I would forever fight for her, even when she couldn't and I hoped she knew that.

THE NEXT DAY we were at I-94 Speedway in Fergus, Minnesota and the reality of what was happening next week was weighing on everyone.

The atmosphere in the pits was much the same. The grandkids were running around, careless and free of any obligation, including listening. I don't know how many times I told Jack to watch where he was running. Twice he was nearly hit by a car coming off the track and I had to pull him out of the way.

"You need to watch where you're running, bud. These guys can't see you in the cars."

He shrugged, cherry lips pulled up in a toothy smile. "I know."

He clearly didn't know because it didn't fucking stop him from doing it again ten minutes later.

"Take them in the stands," I told Lily, annoyed him and Jonah weren't listening to me.

She did immediately, only to have them both start crying.

"Why did you do that?" Sway asked, feeling bad for them.

"I told them twice not to run out of the hauler like that, and they're not listening." I set my helmet inside my car as she approached, wrapping her arms around my waist. It was so fucking hot I couldn't believe she was down here, let alone wearing jeans. "Aren't you hot? Maybe you should go inside the motorhome for a little bit. I'll turn on the generator and get it cooled off for you."

Standing on her tiptoes, she kissed my cheek. "I'm fine, and you're cranky."

I was. "I know... I'm sorry."

The throaty rumble of a sprint car caught my attention on the track. It was Rager breaking the track record like the wheelman he'd become. I'd never regret adding him to the team, even if he had eyes for my daughter.

Sway and I walked hand in hand up to the fence line, the sweet smell of methanol burning our eyes while chunks of clay kicked up from his rear tires as he rode the cushion through turns three and four.

"Man," Sway whistled. "He's flying tonight."

"Yeah," I agreed, shaking my head. "He's gonna make me work for it though."

A giggle beside me drew my attention to her. "I know something you don't have to work for later."

"Mmmm." Kissing the side of her face, I pulled her closer only to have her push away. "Nope, it's too hot for hugs."

"You just said you were fine, and I wouldn't have to work for it later."

"Yeah, you won't. I'll just get on my knees. No touching involved."

"Wow, you make it sound so romantic." I snorted with a laugh.

"Oh, it will be." Her eyes drifted to the pits when Rager was back, everyone around his car congratulating him.

"What's with him and Arie?" I asked as we walked back over to them.

She leaned in, her voice low. "She and Easton are having problems, and I think she's turning to him for answers."

I whistled lowly. "That can't be any good."

"He's a good guy, Jameson."

"E or Rager?"

"Both."

"Uh-huh."

I wasn't sure what was going on with E these days, but I knew deep down Arie and Easton were never meant to be. I wasn't stupid either; I'd known for years she had a thing for Rager, as did most girls.

Rager dominated the night, winning his heat and the trophy dash. Once the feature was underway, there was no catching him. I couldn't even get a peek at an opening to get around him. I ran the top hoping I could find grip up there, but it wasn't happening, and I could barely see a fucking thing with all the dust. Side-by-side with him in the corners, I just couldn't make it stick. I also kept bouncing off everything. Could barely keep the car off the wall. No doubt, I was lucky I finished where I did.

When the race was finished, I stayed back until his interview finished and then congratulated him.

"So you couldn't get past this big guy here, could ya?" the announcer asked me.

"He found the rubber before I did," I told them, giving Rager a hug with one arm. "I should have moved down sooner than him. I made too many mistakes and bounced off the wall I don't know how many times." I shrugged, winking at Sway, who made her way over to us. "Just wasn't my night."

Rager leaned forward and took the microphone from the announcer. "This win goes to Sway." He swung his arm around Sway, kissing her cheek. "You keep this entire operation going, for him, for us." Leaning in, he whispered to her, "You're gonna make it through this. You will because we're all here for you. You can't win a race without your crew," Rager told her softly, winking.

Sway smiled and whispered to him, away from the microphone. "I have no doubt I will. Someone has to keep the boys of JAR Racing in line."

When she leaned into my side, I threw my arm around her, my fingers curling around her chin so she was looking at me. I should have said something. But I didn't. Words weren't needed anymore. She knew exactly what I was thinking.

CHAPTER EIGHT —JAMESON

Flash Shield – A device to encompass the air inlet of a carburetor's sides, top, and rear to protect the drive in case of engine backfire.

I'D DEALT WITH death but never dying. Even though I knew when Charlie had been diagnosed with cancer, I was gone so often it wasn't like I watched him die. Sway did, though. And when he finally did pass, I was in Daytona racing. When we lost Ryder, I didn't know until he had already died. The same could be said for the plane crash and even my own dad's death. So yeah, I had dealt with way too much death, but up until then, I had never faced the possibility of having to stand by and watch someone I loved and cared about die.

While I knew she wasn't dying, it still felt that way at times. At every doctor appointment, it was if they were preparing us for the possibility. Which was probably why I wasn't allowed at the appointments any longer. I couldn't handle the idea of them preparing us for anything other than my wife living through this.

I also hated to be out of control. No race car driver did. But it was all I seemed to know since Sway's diagnosis. Out of control and dependent on one outcome.

Staring at the track in front of me, its grooves and cushions, my life, our life, resembled it in so many ways. We had ruts. Hell, we had down right ditches in some of our wide sweeping turns, but we made it around the track each lap. When would that end though?

I carried speed for so many years. Had we finally hit the brim and blown a tire?

I wanted to be alone the morning of the concert so I snuck out across the street to our dirt track. I wasn't out there long and Tommy found me.

Tommy sat beside me on the bleachers, handing me a new bottle of whiskey. "Wouldn't want you to run out." And then he motioned to the track. "Remember when you went off turn two and into the pond a couple of years ago?"

"Yeah, I had fish in my helmet." Glancing at the bottle, I squinted into the sun, my head throbbing. I didn't say anything. I didn't want to say anything to anyone. Hell, I didn't even want anyone with me.

In fact, I didn't even want to be doing it at all, but for her, I would. For weeks, Arie and my sister had been bugging me to make the night before Sway's surgery special for her. And while I agreed it should be special, I didn't want to do a concert for her. I wanted us to spend the night alone. While that was me, Sway wanted her family around, and I could understand that.

"Where's Sway?" Tommy asked. "This party's for her, isn't it?"

"At the zoo with the kids," I mumbled, my head pounding with every word. I had a headache that started months earlier, a nagging one that never seemed to ease at all.

When I didn't say anymore, he eventually asked, "You gonna be okay?"

"I will if you stop fucking talking." I grunted, leaning back on the bleachers to stare up at the sun. Breathing in deeply, the rays warmed my face, the humidity in the air hovering like dust.

"I'm gonna let that comment slide because I know you're going through something right now, but I think we both know that you secretly love my ability to talk constantly without any real thought to what I'm saying or what the consequences might be." He waved his hand around, spilling his drink over the front of him. "But hey, you know, I'm really going to miss Sway's tits," he said, nonchalantly glancing over at me.

I raised an eyebrow and he scooted away a few feet. "Are you trying to piss me off?"

"You're not thinking about the surgery now, are you?"

Groaning, I scrubbed my hands over my face. "I don't want to talk about the fucking surgery."

"Okay, well then let's talk about that summer because you know, those were some of the best memories of my life."

I knew exactly what he was referring to. *That summer*. It was the summer that everything else in my life compared to. The one where I lost myself, fell in love and found my passion for a sport that dictated my entire life.

"Stay,"

....

"Have you ever thought about this before?" I whispered into the eerie silence of the room knowing she could hear me. My voice soft and soothing as my lips danced across her skin.

"Thought about?"

"This...." My arms tightened around her, kissing her skin once more.

"Yes, and no," she told me.

...

"Sway Marie Reins... I promise to love you every moment of forever... will you marry me?"

...

I reached the point where I couldn't sit there any longer with Tommy. Mostly because I couldn't stop thinking about everything that could go wrong and also, the bottle was empty. When I was back at the house, the girls were back, and my mom was keeping Sway upstairs so she didn't see anything.

Arie saw me and was immediately in my face, accusingly, telling me not to punch anyone. No way could I agree to that. Walking around to the stage, I noticed Dylan and Grayson had arrived so I decided to go thank them for coming.

"It's good to see you, man," Dylan said to me, clasping his hand on my shoulder. He smiled, and I wondered if he remembered me nearly kicking the shit out of him when he was a kid for looking at my wife's ass. Probably. That kind of shit stayed with you.

"Yeah, it's been a few years, huh?" I took another drink of my whiskey. No wonder I was feeling pretty good. I'd bypassed the beer completely. "How're the girls doing?"

Dylan not only married that girl he brought around back in the day but had three girls with her. Immediately, he whipped out his phone to show me pictures. "They're good. Henley's in high school now so I spend most of my time chasing the no-good little fuckers away from her."

"Ah, yes." Laughing, I leaned into the stage, the whiskey kicking in. "I remember those days." My eyes drifted to my only daughter, flirting with Rager. Yep. I remember those days all right. Squinting into the setting sun behind his shoulder, I asked, "How's Bailey?"

"She's doing good." He nodded, reaching for his guitar to adjust the strings. "Started her own gallery a few years back. She really wanted to come out too but couldn't make it. Our youngest is a bit of a handful."

I waved him off. "No worries. I can't tell you how much I appreciate you guys coming on such short notice."

Dylan cleared his throat, his eyes dropping to his feet as if he knew what it took for me to say that, and maybe had an idea of what I was going through. "Wouldn't have missed it for anything."

As much as I didn't want to be doing this, parties just weren't my thing, when I looked around at everyone there to support my wife, I understood the meaning behind the night.

Feeling the emotions rise, I cleared my throat and stood straighter. "Let's look over the playlists."

Dylan smiled and handed me the setlist.

JUST AS THE sun set, Sway came downstairs to her favorite song playing. "It's Time" by Imagine Dragons. I couldn't imagine what was going through her head when she saw me up on that stage, singing to her. My heart raced, waiting for her to approach, and when she did, it took my breath away. She wore a skirt and a black shirt that reminded me of the night in Charlotte. The way she looked up at me, it was if I was right there again, in the doorway touching her, waiting for her to make the first move.

I smiled widely when I saw her and leaned into the microphone to sing to her. Sure, there were like a hundred people here, but I sang for my wife to show her how much she meant to me.

Immediately I saw the tears in her eyes when she was close enough because she knew the meaning behind this song.

....

"Do you remember that night after the race in Charlotte when this all began?" Her arms wrapped over mine, which were around her as though she was cuddling into a warm blanket or a sweater that was soft to the touch.

"I do, honey," I smiled, remembering the overpowering anxiety about what I wanted that night, a night I would remember forever. "I remember the exact look in your eyes when I asked you to stay."

"Me too," she whispered, pulling my hand to her lips, kissing the promise I made to her.

....

When Sway was at the stage, front, and center and began cheering me on like I was a rock star, I laughed in the middle of the song, which caused everyone else to as well.

"Fucking hot!" she mouthed to me, reaching out to grab my leg. I did kinda feel like a rock star right then.

I did everything I could to make the night special for her, including playing all of her favorites. I knew I needed to include "Purple Rain," but just like our lives, it needed to be perfectly placed and anticipated through the night. I knew she was waiting for it, too. I could see the disappointment when we started it, and I moved to "Beautiful Ones" instead.

With my head down, staring at my feet as the music faded, a slow drumbeat picked up into "Purple Rain" and everyone started to scream.

I had her on the stage with me when she recognized the beat. Her hand flew to her mouth as she openly gasped, tears falling slowly. "I love you, so much!" she whispered, shaking her head slowly as if she were in complete awe at my performance.

What really got her was when I dropped to my knees before her, to sing the chorus, my voice echoing through the field, as raw and emotional as our love.

When the song ended, the slow drumbeat faded and the stage went quiet and dark with only us illuminated by a spotlight. Memories bombarded me. Well, one memory really, of the first night I sang this song to her as we danced. The night I asked her to stay. It was our true beginning, and suddenly it hit me. I had been contemplating what to do for her that would mean something more than an "I love you." Spencer mentioned renewing our vows and at first, I didn't think she'd want to. But then I remembered, this was Sway. She may not like weddings, but she loved what they meant, and this was something she'd surely appreciate, my devotion to her.

I was still on my knees before Sway, tears in my eyes when I took her hand in mine. "This night was for you, honey. Just for you. I hope you see how much we can't live without you. And I hope that you'll give me another twenty-five years to show you. Marry me?"

Sway laughed, looking at me like I was insane. "We're already married, Jameson."

Shaking my head, I smiled through the emotion. "I mean again. You...." Despite my attempt not to, my voice broke, and my head fell forward, my shoulders shaking. I couldn't hold it back any longer. It all hit me at once. I couldn't even look at her.

Her hands ran over my shoulders, went to my head and angled my face to look up at her.

When I found my voice, it was shaking. Reaching up, I took her hand from my shoulder placing it over my heart. "There's something here... and it's something nothing else compares to." She knew what I was referring to, her smile so bright it blinded me. "It's worth all the tears and aches in the world to believe in. A man and woman in love. Marry me, all over again?"

Yanking me up, she jumped into my arms. "YES!"

Once I was alone with her, and not on stage, I drew her in close, slow dancing away from the rest of the crowd as Dylan and Grayson took over playing for the night.

"Did you enjoy yourself?" I whispered in her ear, placing a kiss right below her ear.

"I did." She sighed, sinking into my hold on her. "You sounded amazing out there."

"Oh yeah? Why don't you show me how good I sounded," I hinted, waggling my eyebrows.

She gave a nod behind the stage. "Remember that night behind the billboards?"

Fuck, how could I ever forget that night? "Want me to steal your panties and shove them in my pocket?"

Sway threw her head back in laughter. "Who says I'm wearing any?"

Once again, she had the upper hand.

FLASH SHIELD · SWAY

MAYBE IT WAS the heat of the night, or just that my husband was so hot, but I had to have him. My theory was if I was going into surgery tomorrow, I was going to make the most of this night and what he gave to me.

Jameson's hands shook, unsure what I was getting at when I shoved him against the side of the stage. Hard I might add.

It seemed crazy and unlike two people who had kids, and grandkids to be fucking against a stage in the middle of a field, but damn it, we were still young at heart. I would prove it.

There was a reason *why* I fell for Jameson Anthony Riley all those years ago.

There was a reason *why* I married him.

It was essentially because he was a dirty fucking heathen and about to give me one hell of a night against this stage. I knew it when he flipped me around and pulled my hair. "Is this what you want, dirty girl?"

I remembered words we said to each other back then like it was yesterday, so I decided to play a little.

"Jameson," I breathed when his mouth went to my shoulder. "We should probably get back," I teased. I didn't mean it at all.

He growled against my skin, the roughness of his jaw scraping over my sensitive skin. "No. I *want* you. Right now. Like *this*." His wet, cool mouth moved from my lips to my jaw, down my neck and then bit down on my shoulder. "And you shouldn't have worn this skirt." Taking a fist full of the fabric, he pulled it up so it was around my waist and then dropped his hand to my hips to find I wasn't wearing any panties.

Looking back at him, his grin took over, crooked and captivating. A sense of familiarity seeped into me recalling that night against the billboards at Grays Harbor.

I wasted no time when he turned me around so my ass was seated on the edge of the stage, my legs wrapped around his waist. The base of the song playing behind us amplified my emotions as I brought his lips to mine.

Something happened when he kissed me though. It happened to both of us. Immediately, we were a tangle of hands racing to find each other and breathing heavily, much like we were twenty-some years ago.

What would have made it perfect would have been the sound of sprint cars behind us, but The Eagles' "Life In The Fast Lane" worked too because we were in the fast lane.

Jameson unbuckled his belt and then his jeans, pushing them down just enough to free himself, gliding his hand from base to tip twice. I always loved when he touched himself. *Fuck*. It got me every damn time.

There was part of him teasing me. I could feel it. He wanted to make me beg, see how badly I wanted it.

He raised an eyebrow. "Can you put your leg on my shoulder?"

I stared down at the position of our bodies and the potential to fall on the uneven ground. "Probably not." And then I sighed. "Are we getting too old for this?"

"Fuck no." Shaking his head, he spread my legs a little further. "Don't overthink this. We haven't lost anything."

I knew we hadn't, but still, I wanted to fuck him like I used to, all wild and out of control but there had to be some limitations now. Damn old bodies.

As he entered me, he whispered against my heated skin, "I love... so much...." With the tenderness behind them, tears welled in my eyes, overcome by this, him, us, what he did for me. His hands moved to my ass while both my legs curled around his waist tighter, my heels into him, feeling him flexing forward.

I watched the movements in his chest, his stomach, the look on his face, the way he gazed down at me, so in love. Kissing me deeply, sliding in and out as he tried to keep himself steady holding me against the stage with his movements. It wasn't easy, but the friction was exactly what I needed.

The fire inside me built quickly up my thighs and into the pit of my stomach as my orgasm hit me. I lay back against the stage, my eyes on the stars as the pleasure raked through my body. Jameson hunched forward in a desperate attempt to hold off his until I was done.

My knees would have buckled at how good this was, how badly I needed him, but I was captured by the night's sky. Thousands of stars shined down on me, patterns I couldn't make out, but I knew then I'd be okay. Something told me I would.

His pace quickened when I moaned into his ear, shaking around him, frantically clawing at his shoulders to keep him near me. My heart beat against his, thumping wildly in my ears.

He made just two more movements before his body tensed, his back tight, fingers digging into my ass as he drove into me once more.

"You have no fucking idea how sexy you are," he breathed, slumping against me and the stage. His hands and arms still shook as he tried to control his breathing.

Kissing the side of his face, I cupped his cheeks and made him look at me, the sky lit behind him. He looked at me, flushed skin under the moonlight, swollen lips. "Do you feel dirty now?"

Giggling, I kissed him. "I do, thank you."

Jameson always knew how to make everything right. I wasn't sure what tomorrow would bring, but I knew whatever happened, tonight would be with me forever and I had Jameson to thank for that.

CHAPTER NINE — JAMESON

*Force Variation – A process to measure differences in
tire/wheel consistency. Determines the highest portion of the
tread in order to match it up to the lowest portion of the wheel for
best performance and minimize tire/wheel assembly vibration.*

*"I'll be here. Always. Until this stops beating... I'll be here. And
when that happens, you'll be here, with me in my heart until I stop
breathing. If you let go, I'll hold on."*

WHY DID I say that? I wasn't even sure. I even went as far as
sending her dirty text messages all morning of all the things I was
going to do to her when she was better. I guessed maybe it was my
way of distracting the both of us.

They came and told us she'd be heading to surgery in a little
while, and Arie nodded for me to go in.

I must have looked like a drugged man when I came out of
there. I certainly felt like one. If only I had the numbness that
followed. The gravity of the situation, the outcome I could be left
with had sunk in.

"Never give up on our life," she said, her eyes dancing over my
face, memorizing every detail.

Just as the words were whispered to me, it was if they stole my
breath in my lungs. I couldn't do this without her.

Leaning in, I pressed a kiss to her forehead. "You've never known me to give up on anything, have you?"

She smiled tenderly and adjusted her thick white blanket over her chest. "No. I haven't. But it's just a reminder." And then she flipped the blanket back away. "Would it make you feel better if I showed you my boobs?"

My chest shook with an emotional chuckle. "I don't know. Show me and lets find out."

Of course she did, but it was enough to relax me for a minute at least. That was until the male nurse came back to take her away and saw. Given, he'd probably see a lot more during her surgery, I was still half tempted to whip out a sharpie and sign my name over their markings on her. Just so they knew regardless, she was mine.

Narrowing my eyes at the poor kid, I leveled him with a glare. "You look at my wife's chest, and I knock your fucking teeth in."

Turning on his heel, he jetted out of the room.

Sway shook her head. "You're so mean to people."

"He's got no business seeing that." Matter of fact, I'd sign my name after all. Taking the marker they had beside the bed for when they'd made their marks earlier, I decided to let them know just who she belonged to.

She let me do it too, and laughed while I wrote "Property of Jameson Riley" on her chest right below her collarbone.

Property of
Jameson Riley

"There. They should know now." I put the cap back on the marker and tossed it back on the tray.

She rolled her eyes adjusting her gown. "So possessive." Leaning forward, she kissed my nose. "And adorable."

"I love you," I told her, feeling the emotion creep up, the lump in my throat rising when the doctor rapped his knuckles against the door.

Sway's emotion surfaced too, eyes filling with tears. "I love you, too. Now go wait for me. I'll be out of the garage here soon."

My shoulders shook with light laughter as I stood from her bed, her hand slipping from mine as I winked at her.

As she was being wheeled away, I flashed another glare at the nurse, a warning. A look of pure fright crossed his features, and at once, he darted the other way.

I KNEW SHE was alive and would pull through, I did, but it didn't stop the disorientation, the frustration that she was in the hands of someone else.

I want to be in control. Some would say I was a control freak, and I wouldn't disagree with them. Most race car drivers were. It was usually the reason they enjoyed it so much because they were controlling the uncontrollable. Speed.

My mind flooded with memories, ones of us younger, invincible, living on the edge of being out of control.

...

"Sway," my voice was failing me. "Don't go, please," I begged. I wanted her to look at me; then she'd see that I didn't want Chelsea, but she refused, making a vital effort not to see me.

"Why?" Her shoulders shrugged. "Why should I stay?"

"I ... don't want you to go," I admitted. "Not like this."

She let go of my hand and leaned against the counter, her back still to me. "Why, Jameson?"

I had a temper, that was no lie, but when it came to Sway— and letting her go—I knew no bounds. I lost all bearing and threw the piston toward the wall.

"Fuck, Sway," I tried to control my voice and keep from yelling at her, but it was useless. "What do you want me to say? Just fucking tell me what you want to hear and I'll say it. I'll say whatever you want me to!"

...

"Is she ...." I couldn't finish, gasping.

Please tell me she's still alive! Please tell me my angel is still breathing!

"Son, they are doing everything they can for her and the baby." His face was solemn. "I'm sorry."

"Dad," I warned.

He closed his eyes for a long moment before speaking in a low, strained voice. It was hard for him, too.

"For now... they are both... stable." He took a deep breath.

He didn't look very fucking convincing. If there was ever a point in my life where I thought enough was enough, it was right then. I couldn't handle this. I couldn't.

...

"Jameson!" Sway growled. "You need to knock that shit off."

"It doesn't fucking matter anyway," I mumbled inertly.

"Why not?"

"It just doesn't." I fumbled with the hem of my shirt. "The season has already gone to shit. I want it to be over with."

"Jameson Anthony Riley, you need to stop this and pull yourself together!"

"How?" I shouted back, instantly regretting the tone of my voice.

"Okay...." Sway paused for a long moment, and I knew she was pissed. *"I will put up with a lot of shit from you, Jameson, but I will not sit back and watch you throw your career away because of that douche bag. I've been by your side, watching, waiting, and supporting you through it all. So for you to give up now, what does that say about us? What does that say to our son?"* Sway's rant stopped briefly as she sighed. *"I can't watch you do this... I won't sit back and watch you do this to yourself. I get it... I really do. I feel the pain as well. I know how this has left its mark on us, but I can't let it destroy me. We can't let it destroy us. If we do... if we let it destroy us, he's won. They've won."*

...

So many times she had brought me back to reality. But I couldn't do the same for her. All I could do was wait for someone else to tell me if she lived or died.

"Dad, are you okay?" Arie asked, drawing my attention from my thoughts.

"I've...." I took a shaky breath, my chin shaking. Fuck, I couldn't even keep it together for a few minutes. "She has to come through this. I could never do it without her. I can't do this without her. I'll never make it. I don't care what they take from her as long as they give her back to me."

Rubbing my back, she tried to calm my dismay. "The doctors are hopeful everything will be fine. We need to feel the same, Dad."

I couldn't. I just... couldn't.

IT WAS THREE hours into the surgery when a doctor came out. Couldn't tell you what he looked like because all I heard was the word complication.

Sitting up, my uncertainty made my voice harsh and demanding. "What the fuck do you mean complications?"

His eyes widened as he stepped back. "She's fine. It's just taking a lot longer than we anticipated."

"Well say that," I shot back, a heavy dose of sarcasm in my tone. "Don't fucking come out here saying there're complications when it's just taking *longer*."

What kind of fucking doctor was he?

"You don't have to swear, sir," he balked, clearly offended by my sharp response. "And please keep your voice down."

Was he serious? Did he think I would?

Leaning forward, I stood so I could be eye-level with him when I said, "Fuck. You. Get. Back. In. There. To. My. Wife."

Arie pulled me back to her, waving the doctor off. "I'm sorry. Ignore him."

Sitting down, I confessed my frustrations for this place and their lack of grace when it came to dealing with families. I mean, who said that? "These doctors are ridiculous," I complained, my heart pounding as I ripped the words out impatiently. "Who says that shit?"

"I'm sure they're trained to say that," she told me, trying to hand me a sandwich she'd bought for me.

"Well, fuck them," I grumbled, rolling my eyes and pushing the sandwich away. "They need better training."

I stood to leave, tossing the sandwich aside only to have Casten follow me. "Wait up, old man."

"She's going to be fine, dad," Casten told me, seeming confident in his answer.

"You don't know that," I mumbled from my place on the floor in the hallway. "Shit goes wrong all the time."

"Yeah, but this is Mom we're talking about."

I stared at him, waiting for him to explain, but this was also Casten. Maybe he was trying to get me to understand by his cryptic bullshit he always pulled.

"Think about it." He sat down with me. "This is the same woman who at eighteen packed up and traveled an entire summer with you, jumping from town to town, race to race and never even batted an eye. The same woman who was assaulted and pushed down a flight of stairs while pregnant and still managed to not only survive but deliver a healthy baby. I'm not saying Axel isn't a little different at times, but still healthy."

I snorted, shaking my head at his reasoning.

"Oh, and don't forget when she sat by your bedside for weeks not knowing if you were going to live or die. And when you did wake up, she was the one who stood by you through all of your recovery and rehab." Casten laughed once, his head resting against the wall. "And believe me, it was difficult. You were a real asshole then."

I glared at his remark but couldn't help the smile. He had a point.

"Mom survived the death of both of her parents, lost friends, watches her husband and sons risk their lives every weekend on a track. And hell, let's face it, being married to you for all these years hasn't always been a picnic. There's no way something like cancer is going to beat her now."

Casten was right. Sway was the strongest person I knew and if anyone could beat this, it would be her.

"THE DOCTOR CAME by," Arie told me as I returned to the waiting room.

"Which one?" I looked over at her only to stare at the wall beside her. "The one I don't like?"

She snorted. "That doesn't really narrow it down. There's like a hundred you seem to hate."

Rolling my eyes, I slouched in the chair. "What did they say?"

"That it was taking longer, they took more than planned and now they're starting the reconstructive surgery."

I couldn't sit down after that. Standing, I paced. I felt trapped. The room seemed to close in on me and I had to escape.

With my head in my hands, I prayed again. At that point, I wasn't even sure what I was praying for anymore.

I couldn't sit here again.

Storming back out of the room, I roamed the hallway until I found a vending machine. I didn't know why but I had my mind set on Skittles. I guessed I just needed something else to focus on if even for five minutes and finding Skittles seemed like a good idea. Unfortunately what I didn't realize until I found the damn machine was I didn't have any money on me. Not even a fucking quarter.

"Damn it!" I yelled as I punched the front of the machine. Stupid soft glass. It broke instantly. But feeling my fist go through the glass brought me a sense of satisfaction I hadn't had all day. With all the frustration and fear I was carrying around, I needed an outlet and punching that glass gave me it. And Skittles.

"Shit, Dad." Casten rushed down the hall. "What did the machine ever to do you?" Casten laughed as I picked up the bag of Skittles.

"I didn't have any money." It was the only explanation I had.

"Well, all you had to do was ask." He stared down at the broken glass at his feet. "I would have given you some. You didn't have to go and kill the damn thing."

I shrugged, not caring blood dripped from my knuckles where the glass had cut me.

Casten took one look at my hand and his eyes widened a bit. "Um." He nodded behind him. "Maybe we should go downstairs. You might need some stitches."

Not waiting for me to answer, he grabbed me by the arm and led me toward the elevators.

"Hold on one minute. Don't move." Casten ran back to the vending machine and grabbed a couple of bags of Skittles and some chocolate bars. "Okay, let's go."

"**WHAT DID YOU** do?" the barely eighteen-year-old doctor girl asked in the emergency room as I sat there with my knuckles splayed open.

I stared blankly at the girl stitching up my hand. "Put my hand through a vending machine."

"Uh, why?"

"Have you ever done stitches before?" I growled when she dug the needle in and practically hit the bone. "This isn't home economics class. Pay attention."

"I've done plenty of stitches."

Sure she had.

"Why did you punch a vending machine?"

She seemed hell-bent on getting it out of me, so I said, "I wanted Skittles."

Her eyes darted from left to right, and then at me. "So put money in it."

"Why didn't I think of that?"

It took for-fucking-ever to have her stitch my hand up but thankfully, the time passed and the pager in my pocket alerted me Sway was in recovery, and I could see her.

Though she was groggy, Sway perked up when I came through the curtain in the recovery area. Seeing her smile at me, even though it was obviously a drug-induced goofy smile, I could finally breathe again. She was here and she was going to be okay.

"Look!" And there went the gown.

That same nurse—the one I threatened bodily harm to—came back in as Sway was showing me her bandaged chest. You couldn't see much, and I wasn't too thrilled about her being so anxious to just whip them out, but damn, Sway seemed in a good mood so I let it go.

FORCE VARIATION — SWAY

"**YOU GOTTA STOP** that. I don't want everyone knowing what your tits look like," Jameson said to me once the bandages were removed and I basically showed everyone who came in the room my new funbags.

Rolling my eyes, I stared at the ice water with those little round ice cubes I loved so much. "I don't see why it matters. They're not real."

"I don't fucking care. Stop doing it." His aggravated tone drew my stare to his. "How would you like it if I showed everyone my dick?"

"What... are you just gonna start whipping it out?"

He crossed his arms defiantly over his chest. "Maybe I will."

"Show me and let's see."

Yep. I used his line on him.

He surprised me when he reached for the button of his jeans. "Fine, I'll start with you." And then he literally showed me his crankshaft in the middle of the hospital room.

Even with all of the pain medication they had me on, my body responded to seeing Jameson with his crankshaft standing at attention like it was saluting me.

Unfortunately, Casten picked that exact moment to walk into my room.

"Hey, Mom, I brought you.... Oh Jesus! Oh fuck!" He screamed in such a high pitch that someone walking by would have thought it was a thirteen-year-old girl instead of a twenty-four-year-old man.

"Fuck, damn, fuck! I think I'm blind!" I couldn't help but laugh because he was covering his eyes while trying to find his way out of the room. In the process he tripped over a chair and slammed into a wall.

"Damn it, Dad! Put that thing away. This is *not* okay. I am never going to be okay."

Jameson stood in the middle of my room when Casten left staring at me like "did that just happen?"

Staring at his camshaft, I couldn't help myself. "He seems... scared? Did Casten scare him?"

Of course my comment pissed off Jameson as he zipped his jeans. "Fuck off."

After he tucked everything back in place, I motioned for him to climb into bed with me. I had this overwhelming need to be close to him and it seemed even when he was right next to me, he was still too far away.

Carefully snuggling into his side—the funbags were still pretty sore—I placed my hand over his heart. "I missed you," I told him, trying to snuggle even tighter to his side. I couldn't get close enough.

"Missed me?" He let out a breathy laugh kissing my forehead. "I was a wreck out there."

"I know."

Angling my face so I could look into his eyes, his expression of undying love made my heart skip.

"I know what you mean, though. All this time I was so afraid of the unknown. It was killing me to not be able to control the outcome.

And while you were in surgery, they kept coming out and telling us it was taking longer than expected. I felt like I couldn't breathe."

"Is that when you decided to commit assault on a vending machine?"

He laughed lightly and I couldn't help but smile because hearing his laugh was everything to me.

"I needed Skittles."

"You and your candy."

The room was quiet for a moment, the buzzing from the machines next to me the only sound besides our breathing. Jameson took in a deep breath, his chest rising and then falling slowly. "I don't know what I would have done if you hadn't made it through this."

I knew what he meant because he wouldn't have. I was like his torsion bar stop, holding him in a fixed place. Believe it or not, I could raise and lower his car by using an adjustment bolt. The same went for me. Together we knew the adjustments we needed to make and if that stop hadn't been there, there was no telling what kind of setup we'd be left with.

CHAPTER TEN —JAMESON

Choke Linkage — On a carbureted engine, the assembly of parts that controls a valve that limits incoming cold air until the engine reaches operating temperature and is able to vaporize fuel more efficiently.

VAIL COLORADO
DECEMBER 22, 2028

AFTER SWAY'S SURGERY, the end of the season fast approached and before I knew it, Christmas had arrived. She still showed people her tits, but thankfully, it didn't happen daily anymore. After a few complications with her overdoing it, she healed nicely and you wouldn't even know she had breast cancer. She still went back monthly after the surgery for checkups but she'd just been cleared to come back every six months now. Things were beginning to look up for us.

We renewed our vows a few weeks back, but I wanted something more for her. Something she'd always wanted. A white Christmas in the mountains with around thirty people in hopes to all get along and have a nice holiday.

It was a stupid fucking idea.

But I would also never admit it because it was, in fact, *my* fucking stupid idea to do this. Nope. Never happening.

Truth was, I wanted to give Sway everything she deserved and more. After everything she went through over the summer with the cancer and surgery, she needed to know we were all there for her and with her. Every year she talked about wanting a big family Christmas. What better way to give her that than in the one place she loved to get away to in the winter. Vail Colorado. At least that was my plan.

Turning to Sway, I wanted to brighten my mood. We were flying commercial because apparently, I was full of fucking stupid ideas and thought Sway would enjoy all of us traveling together to Vail. My bright idea only further succeeded to put me in a grumpy mood, but I wanted something to take my mind off the insanity of this idea. What better way to do that than with my wife.

I started out by asking if she wanted to go to the bathroom with me for a little align boring. She shot me down immediately.

"You know you want to." I gave my most convincing voice.

"No, actually I don't." She wouldn't even look at me.

I could be very convincing when I needed to be, so I upped my game by whispering in her ear. "Yes, yes you do."

She pushed me back by placing her palm on my face. "Jameson, I do not want to have sex on an airplane again." Then she gave me the look. "You do remember the last time, right?"

I didn't answer because unfortunately, I did though I tried to block that memory out of us on the plane to Rio and that shithead kid beating on the door.

"*Casten!*" Arie screamed at her brother two rows back from us. "You motherfucker!"

Sway sighed, breaking her gaze from mine. "Don't let them get us kicked off this plane."

"And how the hell am I going to do that? It took some convincing just to get them to allow Arie on a plane.

"That's her own fault. She shouldn't have stabbed Casten with a spork."

Sitting back in my seat and facing forward, I reached for my drink. No way was she letting me in which sucked for me because I wasn't thrilled about the whole family Christmas, regardless of it being my idea. "He probably deserved it."

While I was trying to think of a new angle to get her in the bathroom, I could faintly hear Arie and Casten arguing. I was sure everyone else could too.

"Are you sure it's a good idea that we all go to the cabin. Together?"

"It's an eighty-five hundred square foot house. I'd hardly classify that as a cabin."

Sway had some apprehension when I'd suggested it. As did I. I'd seen *Christmas Vacation* probably a thousand times in my life, and I was sure the Griswold's had nothing on this family. It would be nothing short of a disaster. That was a given.

"But still,"—Sway shifted in her seat to face me, searching my eyes for hesitation—"we have thirty people coming. I'm not so sure this is going to work out."

"You wanted a big family Christmas." I raised my drink in front of me to my lips and smiled. "That's what you're getting."

"A concert, a wedding and a big Christmas." Her eyebrows rose. "What have you done with my husband?"

Finally an angle I could work with. "Come to the bathroom and I'll show you."

"*No.*"

It was going to take some convincing, or wooing on my part because she wasn't budging.

CHOKE LINKAGE — SWAY

WHEN I THOUGHT about a big family Christmas, never in my wildest dreams did I think of a private house in Vail Colorado with our entire family. But that was exactly what Jameson delivered.

I heard screaming from outside not long after the boys had left to go out there. "What the hell are they doing?" I asked, peeking out the window through the snow. It was really starting to come down.

Alley squinted. "Looks to me like it's a snowball fight. Again."

Over the years, Jameson had ensured that I have seen some of the most beautiful parts of this world. Vail Colorado at Christmas was certainly no exception. It had always been my favorite time of year and to see it like this was breathtaking, everything from the log cabin house to the thick fluffy blankets of fresh snow.

"There is no way in hell I'm sleeping in a room next to him." When I turned around, I saw Arie pointing her finger in Casten's face as he tried to bite it. She was so mean to him sometimes.

In this nearly nine thousand square foot house, there were twelve bedrooms and some couches. The boys, like Charlie, Noah, Tommy and even Rager offered to sleep on the couch. Which was nice because someone was going to have to. We managed to get the kids into one room and all the couples in their own bedrooms as well, but they were still arguing about who was next to whom.

Figures.

"Fine," Hayden interrupted them. "We will sleep in the room next to Spencer and Alley. You guys can sleep next to Lane and Bailey."

Arie seemed satisfied. "Fine."

Just as I was taking a deep breath and looking through the house, Jameson and the boys came inside wet from the snow. He shook his head when he got to me. "Fucking Tommy hit me in the head." Snow fell from his hair and into my face.

Laughing, I brushed away flakes off his nose. "Poor baby."

"Come kiss it and make it better?"

"Sure." Taking his hand in mine, we were on the staircase when the doorbell rang.

"Fuck, really?" Jameson twisted and stepped up one step pulling me with him. "Ignore it."

"We can't."

Emma and Alley were walking past the door and stopped, wondering who it might be as well. Jameson, being Jameson, sat down on the stairs pouting.

When I opened the door, I wasn't sure what to think. Standing there were two people who took the ugly sweater thing to extremes. No lie. The woman, shaking snow from her eighties hair and looking to be in her late forties was wearing a bright red sweater with kittens knitted on the front. Only their paws had mittens on them, and their tails had bows. Two bows were conveniently placed over her funbags. Looked ridiculous if you ask me. The man, about six inches taller than his wife, and looking like they could be brother and sister, wore a sweater that was even more disturbing. Frosty the snowman, only his carrot nose was awfully low.

"Oh. My—" I elbowed Emma before she could continue, her eyes on the man's carrot nose.

I turned back to look at Jameson, wondering what he was going to say, barely able to control my laughter. He peeked around me to see them, rolled his eyes and leaned his head against the railing. He mumbled something, but I couldn't be sure what. The couple at the door was rather loud.

"Merry Christmas! You're the Riley family, right?" The woman gleamed, all smiles and big bright white teeth smudged with red lipstick. "Can you believe this weather?"

Fucking weirdos. It's the mountains. At Christmas. Of course, it's going to be snowing.

"It's crazy." I waved to the snow accumulating on the overly large front porch lined with Christmas lights and an assortment of red and white decorations.

"Did you hear about the storm coming in?" the man said, and then they laughed. "But we never mind the storms with a nice fire and hot chocolate."

Jameson groaned behind us and stomped to the kitchen.

I kept waiting for them to introduce themselves, but they never did and wouldn't let me get a word in to say anything. Just kept talking. They did, however, hand us a plate of cookies and homemade hot chocolate mix.

"Who were those people?" Emma snickered when they finally left. "They're awesome!"

Naturally, Emma would find someone who talked a lot awesome.

Jameson returned with what looked to be straight whiskey in a glass with ice. "If their last name is Sloan, we're fucking leaving."

"Jameson." I shoved him back lightly by placing my hand on this chest. "Stop. They're nice people."

"Who the fuck are those people?" Spencer asked, spraying an assortment of crackers and what not flying from his mouth.

"The neighbors," Jameson mumbled, watching them walk away through the blinding snow.

"Fucking weirdoes. Who walks all the way over here in the snow? The house next door is like a mile away." Then Spencer spotted the cookies. "Are those oatmeal?"

Jameson slapped his hand. "Hands off. They're mine."

Spencer gawked at him. "Says who?"

"Me." Jameson ripped the plate from my hand and walked into the kitchen. Guessed he was sidetracked with the cookies and sex wasn't happening.

Emma patted my back. "Let's go bake cookies."

"With what? We forgot to go to the store."

"I'll go," Rosa said, raising her hand as we walked into the kitchen to find Jameson sitting there with the whiskey, cookies, and Spencer.

"Get something for my headache while you're there."

Poor guy. He needed some loving. Reaching for his hand, I placed it on my boobs. "I've got some pain relief for you, champ."

He stood immediately. "*That's* what I'm talking about."

"**WHY DO WE** need Tater-Tots?" Rosa looked back at me when I spoke, giving me that look like I was crazy. I got that a lot from Rosa, but so did everyone else. "Oh, for the kids?"

"No. Tommy." Rosa continued to walk around the aisles picking up random items and throwing them in the cart. "He loves them."

Tommy and Rosa's relationship had always been entertaining to me. They were more like sex buddies than a couple, and Rosa was more of a live-in guest than our housekeeper.

When we got back to the house, we started making cookies with the girls, aside from Arie. She was never much of a baker, but she was trying. Just wasn't making anything that resembled cookies.

Lexi, being a few months pregnant now was taking the eating for two literally while Alley laughed at her. "You don't have to eat for two just yet. The baby is only like the size of a flea."

"Really?" Arie squinted. "That's all?"

"No." Emma shook her head. "You're like fourteen weeks. It's like the size of an apple by now."

Lexi lifted up her shirt to reveal a small bump and pointed at it. "That's either poop or baby." And then her eyes lit up staring at the table. "Ohhh, I love those ones!" She gleamed reaching for the sugar cookie I had just finished frosting.

I slapped her hand away when she started taking them all. "Don't eat them all. Those are Casten's favorite."

Tommy came into the kitchen with Casten, barely able to breathe through his laughter and pulled off his beanie cap slamming it down on the table in an exaggerated motion. "I can't... holy shit. I can't breathe." He grabbed at his stomach as he fell in the chair beside the bar.

"What?" Casten asked and then looked at me as if I should know what Tommy had done. He was an idiot. No one knew what Tommy did besides him. And even then, if you did know what he was up to, his motives were questionable.

"Jameson...." Somewhere between his harsh breathing, Tommy finally was able to speak in a voice we could understand instead of waving his hands around. "He had a headache so I gave him Viagra. Stupid asshole thought it was aspirin."

My mouth dropped open. "The fuck, Tommy! Where is he now?"

"The best part is, he doesn't know." Tommy pointed his finger in my face. "So don't tell him."

I shoved him. "Seriously? You don't actually think he's not going to find out?"

Tommy shrugged. "Maybe not."

I wasn't surprised Tommy did this. He did shit like this all the time.

"Besides"—he put his arm around Rosa, kissed her cheek and then headed for the door—"I doubt he'll complain about having an erection for four hours." He turned to me. "Would he?"

My face heated. "Probably not."

Should make for an interesting night for sure.

LATER THAT NIGHT, they were all waiting to see how long it would take for Jameson to have a reaction to the Viagra, but it turned out the pills Tommy had were expired so he wasn't sure if they'd even work.

Boy was he wrong.

We were in the hot tub, me, Aiden, Emma, Spencer, Alley and Jameson when he kept shifting around and telling me he felt funny. I was already drunk, as was Alley and Emma, and we couldn't stop laughing at him.

His face was all red and he kept blinking rapidly. It was entertaining, but I'd had too many rum and cokes by then not to find everything entertaining.

"Look how well I fill out this bikini with these fake funbags!" I shouted, cupping my breasts. "They look amazing."

"Yes, they do," Spencer commented, smiling.

Alley just shook her head knowing her husband meant nothing by it.

Jameson stared at me. "You take that bikini off and I'm going to be pissed."

Wouldn't be the first time. Or the last.

"Calm down." I patted his head and then brought his head to rest on my chest. "See, they're comfortable."

"About the restaurant" Aiden interrupted Spencer in his hour-long debate about smoked brisket, completely changing the conversation. I couldn't follow what he was talking about, but we had all been talking about buying a restaurant together. A way to secure our retirement I guessed, but we'd yet to decide on the location and what we would serve. Knowing the boys, it was looking like barbecue was going to be the preference. "I think we found a great location in Mooresville. We wouldn't even have to put in a kitchen. It used to be a pizza joint, so they have everything already."

"That's good," Alley said, watching Jameson out of the corner of her eye when he leaned into me.

"We need to go! Right now," he said, standing and it was apparent the Viagra had kicked in full strength.

"Whoa, dude," Spencer laughed. "Didn't anyone ever tell you pointing is rude?"

The next four hours, actually, the next six hours were spent trying to relieve the need he had, and even well into the morning, I didn't think he was satisfied.

I was, well, so incredibly sore. It was like my pit lizard days when I couldn't sit down let alone walk right. I guarantee I walked with a limp the next day. I thought for sure I threw my hip out.

CHOKE LINKAGE — JAMESON

"I CAN'T BELIEVE that asshole gave me Viagra," I told Spencer.

"Tommy drinks vodka out of a water bottle in the pits most days. Is he really someone you should trust to give you medicine?" Spencer shook his head as I figured out the next morning that Tommy had given me Viagra instead of aspirin. I couldn't even say I was pissed because there were things a six-hour erection can provide for you. Good things.

"Good point."

None of us knew what we were doing, but we decided to rent snowmobiles and take them on our own private tour of Vail that morning while the girls did whatever it was girls did in the mountains. I wasn't sure why they rented them to a group of guys like this, but apparently, the family name authorized insanity because he just smiled and handed us the keys. Stupid fuck.

"That was easy," Casten said, smiling brightly.

I had to laugh. Between him and Cole, they'd destroyed more vehicles than Spencer and me, but did that stop us from letting them drive away on one?

Nope.

There we were, lined up on the snow all staring at each other like some kind of *Fast and the Furious* movie.

The first miles were fine, but when they started bumping each other, I could tell the additional insurance we purchased was necessary.

"Why are you going so slow? What happened to Jameson Riley, NASCAR race car driver, huh?" Spencer teased, nudging the front of my snowmobile with his.

"Shut up," I replied, trying to gain some focus. "I had a rough night." More like Sway had a rough night, but still, align boring for six-hours straight took a lot out of you.

"I bet you did there, sport. You're drivin' like a bitch." He smiled, hitting his throttle to pull ahead of me and dodging through a group of trees to shoot out in front of me and Casten and Cole. Aiden was back there somewhere with Axel and the rest of the JAR Racing boys, but it didn't appear like they were racing each other. Just messing around and jumping off hills.

"Did you just call me a bitch?" I shouted, following closely behind Spencer. When I was close enough, I kicked at his legs. "I hope you drive this motherfucker off that cliff."

"You're such a baby when you're not winning." He smiled, and that only pissed me off more. "If you were driving the way you *should* be, you wouldn't be losing," he pointed out.

The only problem with all of this was I wasn't exactly paying attention, and we were heading for a cliff.

"Abort, abort, go to plan B!" he screamed and jumped off his snowmobile.

"Wait... what's plan B?" I asked, turning to look back at him.

I suddenly swerved to the right as I flew over the cliff, slamming to the ground with a loud crash. I flew about ten fucking feet and landed in a snow bank, laughing. Turned out it really wasn't a cliff, more of a hill, but still, it was at least a six-foot drop I just made.

"Was this plan B?" he asked, walking over to me after I slid down the hill.

Standing, swaying slightly, I decided to sit back down in the snow. "Nope. That was definitely plan C," I told him, laughing. "Plan B was bullshit."

"Goddamn, racing snowmobiles!" Spencer yelled, pumping his fists in the air.

"Clearly, we didn't think this through." I stood again, trying to make my way back up the snow bank. "Let's get back before that storm hits."

Most of the boys were back by the time we returned to the rental shop.

Only I didn't see Aiden and Cole anywhere. "Where's Aiden and Cole?"

Anytime Cole was missing, you should be alarmed. Mostly because he was probably stealing something to sell. Loved the kid but he was fucking shifty as hell.

Casten shrugged, reaching up to dust snow out of his hair. "They were heading back before us. I thought they would have been back by now."

Spencer shrugged as well. "I don't see them. And what are we going to tell them? Tell them we hit a dog?"

"That won't work," I told them, groaning as I once again picked up pieces of my snowmobile. "They're not going to buy it."

Spencer seemed undeterred, as always. "Don't be so dramatic."

"This had bad news written all over it. What did you expect to happen?" Casten piped in as he carried a piece of his too.

"How'd that happen?" I asked, smiling at him and noticed he was bleeding from his lips.

Casten grinned. "Axel wanted to race. Couldn't let him win."

Brothers. Always competitive.

When we dropped the snowmobiles off, it was pretty fucking evident what happened to them. It clearly looked like someone rammed into each other before they jumped them off a cliff.

"Whose snowmobile is that?" the teenage kid from behind the counter asked, scratching his head in confusion.

"It's yours," I shrugged. "I rented it from you like three hours ago." I handed him the few pieces that wouldn't stay on and the keys. "They've had a little... damage done to them."

"What the fuck happened?" he gaped at the carts.

"We hit a dog."

"A dog isn't gonna do all that shit," the kid said, pulling a tree branch out of the back of the snowmobile Spencer had been on.

"Are you calling me a liar?" I growled in the kid's face.

"No, sir, but you're going to have to pay for the damage. Your insurance doesn't cover all this."

Smiling now, I handed him my credit card. "I never said I wasn't going to pay for it."

WHEN WE GOT back to the house, the snow had let up, but that damn wind made it nearly impossible to see driving.

"It looks dark up there," Spencer noted as we walked up the steps.

"Those twinkle lights on the deck were annoying anyway," I grumbled, stomping on the stairs to release the snow in my boots.

Spencer snorted, shaking his head at my logic. "Why did you have the place decorated if you didn't like the lights?"

"It has nothing to do with the lights. I just don't like Christmas in general."

"What?" He laughed, removing his gloves and jacket and setting them on the deck out of the snow. "Too cheery for you, grumpy Grandpa?"

I shoved him into the railing. "Fuck you. It's for her."

"For her?" Spencer raised an eyebrow and stood next to me watching the snow-covered trees sway in the wind as it howled around us.

"Yes." I gave a nod toward inside. "For her. She wanted a big Christmas, and I'm going to give it to her."

Spencer looked at me, giving me an understanding smile. "You did good, little brother."

I appreciated the sentiment, but I still had my doubts we were going to survive this shit without some sort of lasting scars.

There were no lights, but lanterns lined the front deck. Once we climbed the stairs to head to the door, there was Gray sitting on her potty chair staring at us. Casten, Axel and the rest of the JAR Racing boys following us onto the deck.

"A little mood lighting, pretty girl?" Casten asked her.

She stared up at me. "Poop," she said, clarifying.

Hayden walked up to Casten holding a candle in one hand. "No power and Cole broke his arm. He's a hot mess." And then she frowned. "I can't find Gray."

Casten and Hayden lost Gray a lot, but she always turned up eventually. Casten pointed to the corner of the deck where his daughter was quietly trying to poop outside. "She's cute, huh?"

Jack walked out and then covered his nose with his sleeve of his sweatshirt. "What's that smell?"

And then Abigale, on Rager's shoulders asked, "What's she doin'?"

Gray glared at them. "Poop!" she screamed until the vein in her neck popped out.

"Cole! Stop fucking moving so I can finish putting the tape on it!" Spencer yelled from the family room where most everyone seemed to be gathered tending to him when we walked inside the house.

When we went in there, I took in the sight before me: Sway sitting on an ice pack and Cole with his arm wrapped up with Duct Tape with a bottle of whiskey in the other.

"Did he really break his arm?" Casten asked as I sat back smiling. I didn't know why I found it all amusing, but I did.

"Appears that way."

"Why is Mom sitting on an ice pack?"

"None of your business." I slapped his chest. "Now come help carry firewood inside."

The weather report indicated the snow would be returning and wouldn't quit anytime soon nor was the wind. We'd be lucky if the power was back by Christmas tomorrow.

CHOKE LINKAGE — SWAY
DECEMBER 25, 2028

I NEVER THOUGHT I would be sitting on an ice pack on Christmas morning, but when the warning said an erection lasting more than four hours should be seen by a doctor, I knew I was in trouble. Because I finally understood that warning was not for the user but for the poor crankcase it was using. Last night that warning meant nothing.

Not when you were married to Jameson Riley. We took advantage of it. An entire night and early morning of align boring. This mama wizard needed that so badly. There were times over the last six months I thought we'd lost that, which was why I wanted to do it on the hood of his Mustang, or behind the stage at the concert. All of it reminded me of how we started and that no matter how many times the caution flag was waved and we ran pace laps, we could always find our speed again on the restart.

"When are you going to get off that ice pack?" Hayden asked.

I took another bite of my delicious cinnamon roll Alley made and then took a sip of my mocha. Tasted like heaven. "When my crankcase stops hurting."

Hayden rolled her eyes watching Gray carry down her potty chair looking for a private place to poop. "This family and their terms."

"I know." I beamed, barely able to keep from breaking out into a full-blown giggle. "It's great."

Jameson came into the kitchen, smiling. "Morning, honey." It was a suggestive "morning," one where I was willing to forgo my soreness and run upstairs with him and ask him to slap my tattooed ass and pull my hair. All of which he did the night before last, and did well.

"Morning." I smiled back at him and laughed when Hayden rolled her eyes again.

It was a great morning. Again.

He winked down at me, eyeing my ice pack. "You okay?"

"Feeling good. Just a pit stop." It seemed Jameson's sex drive had been kick started by the Viagra. Now it was like he was racing in the 24 Hours of Le Mans.

Licking his lips slowly, his head dipped forward to the hollow base of my throat where he placed a lingering kiss. "Don't take too long."

"When do you think the power will come back on?"

"Hopefully soon. I want that Christmas prime rib Dad makes, damn it." Casten actually sounded angry over it as he entered the kitchen where we were gathered.

Axel came into the kitchen too, Lily right behind him, and spotted the coffee we made by hooking up the generator to the espresso machine. "Oh, thank Jesus, coffee."

"He uses a propane smoker," I told Casten when Jameson was in the fridge digging out the prime rib. "It doesn't need power so I'm assuming he can cook it."

Jameson gave a nod outside to the steam rising off the back deck. "Yeah, smoker's already going."

"Dad!" Jack came into the kitchen wearing his helmet, something he did often looking for Axel. "Are we going to make it back in time for the Chili Bowl?"

"Yeah, bud." Axel placed his hand on top of the helmet. "We will."

Jack wanting to race bigger cars was a constant battle between Axel and him, as it was with him and Jameson when Axel was younger. Eventually—with Axel—we just gave up and allowed him to race but Jack was little, and I completely understood their hesitation with it. He was only six.

"I know." He frowned. "But if Grandpa Jameson wins, I get his helmet."

Ah, yes. The helmet collection. It started with Jameson collecting helmets in the showroom of JAR Racing and eventually Jack started one too. I found it adorable our grandson wanted to be just like his father and grandfather. They were both good men to look up to.

Casten laughed when Jack ran back into the family room. "It's hard to get him to focus on anything but racing, huh?"

"Pretty much," Axel noted, dishing himself a cinnamon roll only to have Jonah take it from him.

Just as the boys were talking about another snowball fight outside, Jameson came in from the garage carrying the prime rib already seasoned. Placing it on the counter, he reached for the 6-pack in the fridge he used in the smoker to keep the meat from drying out.

He smiled, proud of his abilities to make the best prime rib I've ever tasted. "Ready for dinner in about ten hours?"

"You guys are going to open that restaurant, right?" Casten asked. "And can you serve this every day?"

"Why?" Jameson didn't look up from the roast as he rubbed more garlic around the outside. "You're not in town *every day*."

"True. Okay." He considered his request again. "How about the 'Casten Special' and I call ahead when I'm in town."

Chuckling, Jameson placed foil over the roast and carried the plate to the door. "I'll see what I can do." He stopped at the door and pointed outside. "Casten, she's going to get sick out there."

Casten and I stood to see who he was talking about. It was Gray, on the deck with her potty chair sitting naked on it watching the snow.

"She's a free spirit." Casten offered proudly, but essentially, she was just that. Perfect kid for him.

"Why is that kid always naked and sitting on that chair outside?" Aiden asked, coming into the kitchen right behind Spencer.

"She takes after her father. Casten was naked most every day until he was five," Jameson added, "And where the hell were you last night?" he asked Aiden.

No one knew what happened to Cole and Aiden during the snowmobile adventure; just that Cole somehow broke his arm, and Aiden felt horrible about it.

"I was racing with Cole," Aiden explained, sitting at the table, his eyes widening as he remembered the incident. "Something went wrong and I ran over him."

"I see." Jameson tried not to smile, but it was useless. He couldn't help it.

It was pretty funny that he ran over him because if you knew Aiden, he was always so cautious. Never drive anywhere with him. Ever. It was like driving Miss Daisy around.

"Are you okay?" Spencer asked him.

"No, I feel sick." Aiden's head fell to his hands. "He could have gotten really hurt by that."

"Oh, don't beat yourself up too much. He's fine." Spencer grinned. "And Tommy can help you out. I hear he's got some anti-nausea pills."

"Really?" Aiden perked up.

"Yep." Spencer nodded.

And off Aiden went to find him. Stupid fucks.

Soon after Aiden left to find Tommy, Cole walked in looking like total shit. No, I take that back, he looked totally wasted.

Looking around the kitchen to see if I was the only one who noticed he was obviously using again, only to be distracted by Jameson returning from the smoker and placing his lips up against my ears.

"So I have some time… wanna do a little press forging upstairs?"

"As good as that sounds, I need a tiny break."

His brow lifted. "How long of a break?"

"Another night?"

He groaned and flopped into the chair next to me. Watching Cole closely, I nudged Jameson with my elbow. His head popped up immediately only because he thought I changed my mind.

"Is Cole high?"

Skewing his head to the side, he eyed his nephew. "Probably." And then he looked closer when he grabbed a bag of chips out of the cupboard and took them with him, bloodshot eyes barely open. "Yep."

Great. We had that to deal with. Cole was on a rapid decline to rock bottom. He'd turn his life around for a few months at a time, but it never seemed to stick. For the most part, Spencer tried to get him to grow up, but Alley actually babied him a little. And if you knew Alley at all, you understood how weird that was to think of her being soft with anyone.

LATER THAT MORNING, we finally all got our shit together enough to gather around the tree and hand out the gifts. We had shipped everything the week before we arrived so that the kids would still be able to enjoy Santa visiting them on Christmas.

Sitting on Jameson's lap watching our family together, I was thankful he brought me here for this with the white snow falling, the candles everywhere because the power still hadn't come back on, and Gray sitting in the middle of it all on her potty chair.

Nothing would bring back the losses we'd had over the years, the pain, the voids, but one thing created a small closure. Happiness.

"Having you here with me is the best Christmas present ever," Jameson said in my ear as we watched our kids and grandkids open presents.

I turned to face him, firelight flickering his warm green eyes.

"Thank you," I told him, meaning it with all my heart.

Jameson smiled. "I'm glad you're enjoying yourself."

"No. I don't mean for this."

His brow creased in confusion not understanding what I was saying.

Reaching for his hand, I took it in mine squeezing lightly. "I mean thank you, for *everything*. You've given me an amazing life." He winked, maybe too choked up to say anything himself, so I added. "You made all of this possible and I don't know how I can ever truly thank you for asking me to *stay*."

His chest shook with laughter. "Well, I was naked so I bet the decision wasn't all that hard."

I wracked my brain for a moment remembering that night and if he was naked at the time, but he wasn't. It was in the doorway of the hotel. Believe me, I remember every single detail about that night. "You were not naked when you said 'stay'." And then I remembered that awful skirt Emma made me wear. "I was... kind of."

Shrugging, he had to make his point when he said, "Either way, someone was naked, and staying was *definitely* the better option."

He had a point. "Very true."

CHAPTER ELEVEN —JAMESON

Give up – Gradual or drastic deterioration of a tires performance during use.

SEPTEMBER 2029

AFTER CHRISTMAS, AGAIN, our lives seemed to take a fast lane and early September we were on the west coast. Sway had made a complete recovery from the cancer and remained in remission. I was so fucking thankful for her to be alive and okay I'd laid back quite a bit even and thankfully she stopped showing everyone her tits. It only happened like once a month now.

We started the season strong only to have a string of engine failures. Rager was doing great though and bringing in the wins one by one. Maybe from the temptation of having my daughter around him so much, but either way, it was nice one of our cars was winning this year.

Arie was traveling with us and working part time for the World Racing Group. I had to admit, it was nice having her around that much. Casten was now racing full time with the Outlaws but still hadn't pulled off that first win yet. It was coming any day now though.

Since we were on the west coast, most of our family was around for the last stretch of the tour away from home. Even Jack was here tonight and eating up every moment in the pits he could.

It was on lap fourteen of the feature event when life as we knew it came to a complete stop. The car in front of me had been squirrely in the opening laps but something went wrong on lap fourteen.

Everything seemed to move so slowly, yet too fast. I was moving, doing things, demanding people to react, but I had no control over my own body after I saw it happen. My mind wouldn't comprehend any of it.

I saw the car wiggle in two and then shoot up the high line. I'd had that happen before on my own car and immediately knew his throttle was stuck.

The car did a half-wheel stand midway through the backstretch and then shot up over the barrier and flipped into the pits. I knew who was in the pits right there.

The boys.

When the lights on the track blinked yellow and then red, my chest constricted. I had barely stopped the car on the backstretch before I was out and running toward the pits.

I saw Tommy first, face down in the dirt with Casten hovering over him, and then Jack about ten feet from him under the four-wheeler.

Oh, God. No. Please no. Not him.

My first thought was a few broken bones. When I made it to Jack and flipped the four-wheeler off him, it wasn't broken bones any longer. He was bleeding heavily from his neck.

I couldn't fucking breathe. My breath came out in short quick gasps to keep from fainting on the pure adrenaline racing through me. My heart thudded loudly, my adrenaline spiking, coursing through my veins like ice. My heart pounded, moving through my chest, to my arms, shaking my hands then jolting through my legs.

Amongst the wreckage of the sprint car, Jack had been hit in the neck by something, leaving a three-inch-long gash along the left side of his neck. By the lifeless way he lay there, he was gone already, but I had to try. When I reached him, I fell to my knees beside him. His eyes opened, and then closed, his breathing short and uneven.

I started ripping my gear away, my helmet first, then gloves and the upper part of my racing suit, wanting to use the T-shirt I had under it to press against his neck. His body was completely limp, as though all muscle tone was gone. He almost felt soft, as if all his strength had suddenly disappeared.

"Jameson," Willie gasped when he came over to us, pure white and covered in blood from Tommy.

Two paramedics ran over, their arms full of supplies but stopped, the same blank faces as everyone else when Jack drew in a labored gurgled breath. When he did that, blood pooled in his mouth.

"Do something! Help me! Call 911!" I looked down when warmth hit my hands. The blood had soaked through my shirt in less than a minute, pooling in the dirt beneath my knees. Jack wasn't moving at all, his eyes closed, face pale, lips blue. "Do something!"

"Jameson... he's...." The paramedic shook his head and pressed more towels to the side of Jack's neck.

"No! Don't you fucking give up!" I shook my head refusing to believe my grandson was dying in my arms. "He's not! Just apply pressure. He's going to be fine."

His blood covered me within two minutes. All I saw was red. It was everywhere I looked. It wasn't just coming from his neck either. It seeped out of his mouth. He had to have hit his head, or he was bleeding internally. Everything was happening so fast, and I couldn't stop the blood. He was slipping away right before my eyes.

We used towel after towel, anything we could find to put pressure on his neck, but it soaked through just as fast.

This isn't real. It can't be. He's just sleeping.

"Breathe, buddy!" I touched his face, careful not to move the pressure on his neck. "Fucking breathe!" I sobbed, my face soaked with tears. "Please fucking breathe!"

Watching someone's life slip away before you hurt more than any pain I'd ever endured. I saw the life seeping out of him, the hopelessness taking over.

Make it stop. Make time stop. Make the pain stop right now. Give him life. Take mine. Give it to him. I'll sacrifice the very breath in my lungs if you just please give it to him.

"Jameson," the paramedic said again, grabbing my arm.

I pushed him away, keeping one hand on Jack. "Stop saying my fucking name and do your goddamn job!"

I looked back down at Jack and he was turning blue, his skin a light gray but with a purple tint around his eyes. They were bruising already.

When Sway was attacked, I wasn't there. I couldn't save her. Nothing I could have done would have done or made a difference that day. But now... maybe....

When my dad died, I was dying myself. I couldn't save him either.

But I was here, the first one to Jack and I could save him. I needed to save my grandson. I had to....

I just had to. For me. For Axel.

Only... he was gone before I had the chance.

There was yelling all around us, and guys tried to shield everyone from what was happening not more than thirty feet from the track in clear view of the pit stands. My eyes drifted to Axel as he approached, his helmet in hand. My first-born son took in the sight before him. His first born laying in a pool of blood.

I was afraid to look at Axel. Afraid to see his eyes, but when I did, the pain hit me like a bullet to the chest.

Rager grabbed more towels from somewhere and threw them in my direction. We applied more to his neck but didn't remove the ones that had been soaked through.

Axel didn't move. He just stared at Jack's body. Guys swarmed around him, waiting to see what he'd do as Lane stayed right beside him, waiting.

"Jameson, we need to transport him."

My hands shook. I couldn't let go of him until I realized that he wasn't breathing any longer.

Closing my eyes, I released a sharp intake of breath.

"Jameson...." My name was said by the paramedic. "Let go of him."

Let go of him? How could I? How did this even happen?

The paramedics took over and tried to control the bleeding while another did CPR. I knew there was no chance, but they weren't going to give up on a child in front of his dad. They kept looking to Axel then back at Jack, and then me.

I fell apart when he was loaded into the ambulance. I fell apart because that was when Axel did, his knees hitting the dirt with desperation.

It couldn't end like that. It didn't happen like that for kids.

But it does.

It did.

As I stood there, staring at the ambulance that Axel was getting into behind Jack, I couldn't breathe.

There are no words to describe this pain. There never would be. The pain was not instant. You bled it. It poured out of you, dripping from your broken soul.

And when you finally did feel it, it took the breath right out of your lungs.

Nothing I'd ever been through in my life had resembled this. My grandson had died in my arms.

An indescribable guilt knotted in my chest when I thought about Lily, and then Sway, and Justin, Ami... all our families. This was something that tore families apart completely.

What would this mean for ours?

Handing my keys to Willie, I couldn't even look at him. "Go get my truck for me."

I had no idea what to do next as the ambulance left. I was crying, covered from head to toe in blood and left with a sense of shock throughout my body trying to decipher if I had just watched my grandson die in my arms.

Standing beside the hauler, my knees gave out, my head in my hands as I prayed. "Don't let this be real. Please don't do this."

Each breath seemed harder than the last, a reminder his had been taken.

Casten approached me, his hand on my back in an attempt to comfort me.

Our eyes met for the briefest of moments before I stared at the dirt and climbed to my knees.

"Someone call Lily and Sway," I told him, scrubbing my hands over my face as I climbed to my feet. "Have them go to the hospital."

Willie drove up with my truck. Glancing at Casten, I knew he'd take care of everything here for us. "Can you...?" I couldn't even finish my sentence. It seemed my voice and ability to form words was gone.

"I'll take care of it."

Breathing heavily, my head was light. Words and voices spun around me but I was too numb to decipher who or what anything meant. I knew one thing, we were all heading home now. "Tell the boys to pack up and head home. We won't be at the final two races in California."

I saw the track officials approaching and Arie running toward the pits, but I left with Willie to go to the hospital. Neither of us said a word on the way there, which was a first for Willie because he usually couldn't stop talking.

When tragedy of any kind unfolded around you, there was almost a sense of despondency that took over. It was probably meant to be that way.

Your bodies way of humbling you I supposed.

I STOOD IN the waiting room of the emergency room when they told Axel Jack had passed away. That sensation, the pain coursing through my veins had to be nothing compared to what Axel went through in those seconds the graveness hit him.

I knew what I went through, but to his father, it was completely different. He helped bring him into this world and had to watch him leave it in such a brutal way. This wasn't something where he died in his sleep; he bled to death in my arms. I was covered in that reality.

As Axel's body trembled and he leaned into the wall for support, Sway and Lily came around the corner. I wasn't sure what was said. I was in too much shock to decipher anything at that point. It seemed I wasn't even in my body, let alone watching the devastation unfold around me, my family fall apart.

I'd had so much experience with death, but never directly. When Charlie died, I wasn't there. I was racing, and Sway had to deal with it on her own until I was able to fly home.

When the plane crash happened, it was the aftermath I dealt with.

When Ryder died, I wasn't there. I heard about it a day later.

And when my dad died, I was unconscious, and it saved me from the pain I would have endured then.

But this... I was right in the middle of, watching my son tell his wife their first-born died at the track, bled to death in my fucking arms.

Breathing in deeply, shaking and inconsistent, Sway wrapped her arms around me, crying into my chest. I had no idea how to comfort her like a husband should have because all I kept seeing was Jack's face and the blood on my hands.

This, above all else, would change our perspective on life.

My dad once told me, and this advice became legendary over the years, "It's hard to see past the speed when you're going two-hundred miles per hour."

Those words were never truer as our world had come to a complete halt. We were forced to see what was right in front of us: grief, loss, devastation. It was one long inescapable moment.

"Did you see it happen?" Sway whispered, gasping at my bloody clothes as we stood alone in the hallway.

"Not really." I couldn't look at her. Instead, I stared at her hands on my waist. "I saw the car do a wheel stand on the backstretch. He... died in my arms."

THE HEADLINES A few days after the accident were enough to make me physically sick.

They wanted to say how dangerous our sport was and that it should be illegal to have kids in the pits. The fact of the matter was, he was out of the way of the track, and it was a freak accident. No one could have predicted that would have happened.

Who was to say he couldn't have been hit by a car walking down the street? That happened all the time, but because it was a race car, people went crazy and placed the blame on the sport.

So if I were to die in a car accident, people would still drive cars. They wouldn't outlaw them.

But if I died inside of a race car, they wanted to ban them and put restrictions on everything.

People were so fucking ignorant. They also wanted someone or something to place the blame on.

Sometimes you couldn't. Shit just happened.

They blamed us for what happened.

Why?

Because they weren't there. That was why.

Because a child died and they found it necessary to blame someone. The fact of the matter was it was a horrible fucking accident.

Within a day, we were getting reports that tracks all over the states had immediately implemented new rules to the pits. No kids under sixteen allowed while cars were on the track. If they were racing a premier show, like the Outlaws, anyone under sixteen had to be in the stands before cars could be on the track. It would certainly make it hard on the families traveling with young kids.

There was a pain in the world that would never touch another pain. It didn't even come close.

A child's death.

Our family would never be the same again. This changed us all. Sure, we'd experienced heartache, but never like this.

This could destroy us forever. No one wanted to lose a child. It was unimaginable and avoided in conversation.

The friction it put on everyone was the hardest. Much like Sway's cancer, it created an anger impossible to control, bled a hatred difficult to stop. Only worse.

The thing was, if we collapsed as a family, we wouldn't be honoring Jack's memory. Collapsing seemed selfish and I didn't want that at all.

Everyone wanted to tell us that things happened for a reason. Well, fuck them! This shit should never have fucking happened. Kids weren't supposed to die.

I had no idea what to say to Axel and one look at him that morning, I knew he didn't want to hear anything I had to say to him. He didn't want to hear from anyone.

IN THE MIDST of planning the funeral, Axel decided that having helmets line the top of his casket was what Jack would have wanted. He would have said, "That's so cool!"

We wanted to have all of them up there, but sadly, he was small, so only four helmets would fit. So we chose his favorites: one of Jimi's with the American flag on it, mine, Axel's, and the helmet his parents gave him for his seventh birthday.

Four generations of drivers.

I thought of him right then, in my father's arms, watching us and smiling. The thought provided comfort in a time when I really just wanted to mourn the loss of my grandson.

The morning of the funeral, I was down at the lake sitting on the dock when Sway approached me, wearing the same despondent countenance everyone was.

She said nothing but sat on my lap. Her arms wrapped around my neck tightly. We sat in silence until her lips pressed tenderly to my temple, her tears flowing again.

It brought a surge of emotion over me as the dock rocked with a subtle wind. For twenty-five years we'd experienced more than most could ever conceive of enduring, but this woman in my arms had been through it with me. Cancer, death, plane crashes... retaliation... all of it.

Losing our Jack was by far the hardest.

My arms tightened around her, deep sobs racking the two of us. Words weren't necessary. We both knew the impact this was going to have on everyone.

It was right then that I was reminded of my thoughts when my team plane crashed nine years earlier. I compared my thoughts to a reciprocating engine. It was similar to now. In an engine, there were moving pieces inside that engine, systems that keep it running, belts moving, oil flowing and spark. You could take one out of the equation, and the engine failed. You depended on those systems to keep everything moving.

"Jameson...." Sway's voice brought me from my thoughts. "Are we gonna be okay?"

"I love you," I told her over and over again because the truth was, I didn't know if we would be okay. It seemed almost redundant to keep telling her, but after everything, it was the only thing I could say.

I told her because it's what we needed to remember today. We needed to remember despite the pain and anguish, we could make it through this.

Tears streamed down our faces with an unstoppable force along with choking, bone-rattling sobs.

"I love you, too. You can be sure of that," she assured me with steady palms cradling my face. "This sucks, it's awful, but we have our family here to support us in this red flag."

She was offering me anything she could to provide like she always did. But it wasn't me she needed to comfort. It was our family I cried for the loss, the pain, and I tried like hell to detach myself from the memories, the flashbacks of the night but I just couldn't.

"It's going to be okay," she whispered to me.

"Sway," my voice cracked, remorseful tears falling from my eyes. "I don't know what to do...." My eyes shut, trying to stop the few tears that slipped by. "How are we ever going to come back from this?" I continued, unable to hold her stare.

"I don't know," she finally replied, her voice carrying with the wind.

The truth was, neither one of us were sure anymore.

STAHL

CHAPTER TWELVE — JAMESON

Nosing Over – When a race car's performance "flattens out"
or doesn't pull down the straights anymore. Poor tuning or
exceeding the engine's power range causes this.

MARCH 2030

IT WAS AS if my life was going wide open down a backstretch
with a corner approaching after Jack's funeral in September. The
season ended with little celebration and Rager winning the
championship for the World of Outlaws.

Christmas was quiet, our family struck by devastation and
unable to enjoy the time of year, a vast difference from our time
spent in Vail. We talked about going back, to remember when we
had fun, but nobody wanted to celebrate at the time. I couldn't
blame them.

"He lives his life in the fast lane," a reporter once said about me
during a championship speech. It stuck with me for some reason.

Life in the fast lane.

What did that even mean?

When he said I was living life in the fast lane, he was right
because it seemed regardless of how many times I tried to slow it
down, it didn't work. One thing was for sure, my speed had flattened

out, and I wasn't sure how much longer I could run like this. I had no power left.

Casten came inside the house brushing grass clippings from his shorts. "Sorry. I crashed a riding lawn mower into your garage." Opening the fridge, he glanced at me going over schedules at the kitchen table. "No hard feelings?"

"At least you didn't set it on fire," I mumbled, trying to figure out how I was going to get sponsors for Axel's car this year. Since he backed out at the last minute, I lost two of them, so we had to pick up an extra twenty grand if we were going to make it work.

"Yes, there's that."

Taking out a beer, Casten then left. "I'll go fix the garage door now."

Shaking my head, a small smile tugged at my lips. Casten was different lately. Part of him still felt guilty over everything that happened with Jack, when in reality, he had no control over that night, which in turn made him grow up a bit. Ordinarily, if he crashed into my garage door, he'd laugh it off and make me fix it.

Now he was offering to do it.

When he was out of sight, I looked over the NASCAR schedule. Easton had just won the Daytona 500 and was off to a great start. While that was all good, it made for a slightly busier month for me.

Not long after my dad died, I retired from racing but remained the owner of the team he left to me. I wouldn't say it was because of his death that I retired from racing in that series; it just made me realize how short life was and how much time I was wasting because I wasn't enjoying racing in NASCAR anymore.

Well, I'd quickly discovered that I had to have racing in my life and went back to racing sprint cars where my passion for the sport began. Now with Sway's cancer, and then Jack dying, did I still want all the responsibilities I had?

Not only was I a partial owner in Riley-Harris Racing, but I was still at the shop a couple times a week when time permitted and constantly on the phone with Tate. It took up a great deal of my time. On top of that, I had JAR Racing and CST Engines to run. No way was I giving up those two, so it came down to, "what gives?"

A COUPLE OF hours later, I was still at the table trying to figure out the sponsor snags and the latest penalties NASCAR handed down from the last race in Phoenix when a text from Casten came through telling me to take a look at Easton's commercial. Grabbing my iPad off the counter, I looked it up on YouTube. It wasn't a surprise to me he'd done a commercial. The guys did them all the time. It was part of the deal with their endorsements.

What I didn't like was what the commercial suggested. He's fucking married to my daughter, and the commercial had him making out with some model. I'd done commercials where women were involved, but there was a fine line there and some things I flat out refused to do. Easton apparently didn't care about what image people saw of him.

Just about at the end of the commercial, Sway came inside. "What's that?" she asked when she saw Easton on the screen.

"It's the new Atry Sunglasses commercial with Easton." I gestured to the screen, pausing it. "Have you seen this?"

"Yeah. He really seems to get into the part."

As soon as she said that, I pushed the play button again and wished I hadn't. What the fuck was this crap? "Has Arie seen this?"

"You know Arie. She doesn't talk until she is ready. I'm sure if something is going on she'll come to us." Turning around, she removed a bottle of water from the fridge. "Man, did you hear Alley and Spencer the other night?"

"I don't know what to think other than Spencer is acting like a real asshole lately. I get that he's mad, but he needs to get his head out of his ass and realize that I did him a favor by sending Cole to rehab."

"You need to stay out of it, Jameson. I don't think you should help Cole anymore. This is for Spencer and Alley to handle. They've got a lot going on." She paused, her nose scrunching. "And Cole was arrested again last night."

"Fuck." Sighing, I set the iPad on the table and glanced over at her. "Are you serious?" She nodded sheepishly as if she hadn't wanted to tell me. "That fucking kid just can't get his shit straight. What's it going to take for him to realize what a fuck up he is?"

"I don't think it's a matter of Cole not knowing he's fucking up. I think it's a matter of him not knowing how *not* to fuck up." She stood before me, staring down at me in the chair as she ran her hands through my hair. "Either way, Jameson, you need to stay out of it."

With a heavy breath, my eyes met hers. This woman... she was just so smart and logical about everything. Ever since the surgery, she had an outlook on life that reminded me of my father. So levelheaded. If only I listened to her more.

"I've been thinking of making some changes over at the shop."

Sway didn't look up from cleaning up the mess Casten left in the kitchen when he came in for water. At least he fixed the garage door. Baby steps I supposed. "Oh yeah, what kind of changes?"

"I'm thinking of taking a step back and maybe letting Tate take on more of the responsibility of running the day-to-day of Riley-Harris Racing... or maybe even signing it over to Spencer."

The cup in her hand dropped into the sink, her eyes meeting mine. "What do you mean take a step back? Like retire?"

I couldn't miss the sadness in her voice when she asked that. I wasn't sure I ever would retire completely because it was almost like she couldn't fathom the idea of not having racing in our lives. Honestly, I couldn't either. Racing was and would always be a part of my life. But ownership, it was hard enough running JAR Racing and CST Engines. At some point, something had to give, and since Jack died, I knew what that something was.

"Well, I'll still run JAR Racing and CST Engines... and race of course, but I think it's time I let go of the NASCAR side altogether." She sat down across from me at the table, watching me closely as I poured my thoughts to her.

"Why would you do that? I thought you loved running Riley-Harris Racing?"

I shrugged, shaking my head slowly. "It's gotten to be so much lately and with what's happened in the past couple of years with you and losing Jack, it's just made me think that I'm not getting to spend time on the important things because of my schedule with racing and running the team."

Her eyes flooded with tears the moment I mentioned Jack's name, especially since we didn't see even Jonah or Jacen since Lily and Axel split up. So it wasn't just losing Jack; it felt like we'd lost a lot more.

STAHL

CHAPTER THIRTEEN —SWAY

Pace Lap – A lap just before the start of a race where the pace car gradually brings the field up to a racing speed. The purpose of the pace lap is to prevent big discrepancies in speed between different cars from developing. Having all cars start the race at nearly the same speed makes the start safer. It also gives the engine and tires a chance to warm up.

JUNE 2030

STARING AT THE bowl of gummy dicks, I had to ask, "What the fuck are those?"

Emma grinned proudly. "Jameson infused dicks. Matches his personality great, don't you think?"

We had driven to Detroit Lakes after the race last night at I-96 because someone—that someone being me—had the bright idea to rent a houseboat for a few days to celebrate Jameson's fiftieth birthday. I knew it wasn't a birthday he was looking forward to so, of course, I decided to make a big party with our closest family and friends.

As usual, Emma had taken the lead on the party planning. I was fine with that because to be honest, no one could plan a party like Emma. *I mean Jameson infused dicks?* Seriously, who came up with that shit? Emma did, that was who.

I popped one in my mouth and then let the tiny gummy penis slide between my teeth and showed Jameson, who was walking up to me carrying a case of Coors Light. I held it between my lips with the head sticking out.

"Want one?"

At first, I didn't think he realized what it was until he did and gaped at me. "What the fuck is that?"

I sucked it back in my mouth and chewed slowly. "It's a dick. A gummy dick infused with Jameson." I pointed to his sister. "Em's idea."

Emma hid behind me before saying, "Seems fitting for your personality."

"You're a bitch," he flat out told her, attempting to kick her since his arms were holding the beer. And then he eyed me carefully. "Don't get too used to that dick in your mouth. Mine will be in there soon enough."

Emma pretended to throw up. "That's disgusting."

Alley came by next, both arms full of groceries. "This was a good idea, right? To like, have this party on a boat?"

"*No one* said it was a good idea," Rosa added, following behind her. "It's probably a horrible fucking idea."

Rosa was right, but if we thought about the possible outcome before we did anything, hell, Axel might have never been born.

Jumping the start was what we did in this family, consequences be damned.

Not too long into the day, everyone was already feeling the effects of heavy drinking while sitting out in the sun. Needless to say, we were all shitfaced pretty early on.

"Hey, dick tits," Casten said to Willie, leaning back in his chair. "Get me a beer."

Willie turned to Jameson, who sat in the direct sun with a genuine look of hurt. "Why does he call me that?"

Turning to watch Casten, I could see his grin on his face, enjoying the fact that he was annoying Willie enough that he turned to Jameson for help.

Turning to Casten with a frown, Willie appeared offended for the first time. He took a lot of abuse from the boys of JAR Racing but if you asked me, a lot of what Willie was subjected to was his own doing. "You're making me not feel good about myself."

Jameson shrugged, reaching for another beer and keeping one hand on my thigh. "You want to know what I'm going to do about it?"

Willie actually perked up a little bit thinking Jameson was going to say something to Casten in his defense. "Well, yeah, you're his father. Why don't you act like it?"

Jameson side-eyed Willie and smirked. "I'll tell you what I'm going to do about it... jackshit because I don't give a fuck." With a slow lift of his hands, he shrugged again. "What about that?"

Casten burst into a laughing fit that ended in him falling out of his chair while Willie stood up and stomped away mumbling something about how he was going to find Pork Chop because at least the pig was nice to him. The irony was not lost on me that his only friend was Tommy and his pet pig.

"You shouldn't be so mean to him," I told Jameson, running my hands over his heated shoulders. "And you need sunscreen."

"I need sex," he whispered, giving me a lazy-lidded once over.

"Later." I winked, only to have him roll his eyes. With as drunk as he was, I kinda doubted sex was going to happen.

Things calmed down again after Willie's little emotional outburst, and everyone seemed to be enjoying themselves so naturally, it wouldn't last.

"Casten! Damn it. What the fuck is wrong with you?"

Yep, here we go.

As soon as I heard Arie's scream, I knew Casten was starting his second wave of terror. That was the thing with Casten; he was a ball of energy at all times, and when he wasn't moving, he was thinking, and when he was thinking, it usually led to no good.

"What a shit biscuit," Arie exclaimed, storming past me with what I could only hope was sunscreen sprayed in her hair. If not, what the fuck would it have been? She also had the distinct smell of beer waffling off her which I could only imagine was also a product of her brother.

Minutes later, I heard another scream and a splash followed by Casten, again, laughing so hard I thought he would hyperventilate.

Honestly, I had no idea how he survived all these years. One of these days, he was going to wake up to Arie smothering him with his own pillow, and I doubted anyone would be able to save him at that point. He'd created so many enemies.

Gratefully—after getting pushed overboard—Arie decided to stay in the water, floating close to the boat on a tube and staying far away from her brother.

I would glance over to check on her every now and then, and she seemed content with her little piece of paradise, but it was only when Rager decided to join her that I saw her truly look like she was enjoying herself.

Something was definitely going on between Arie and Easton. It was obvious by the way she not only avoided conversation directed toward their marriage but also seemed to be avoiding Easton altogether.

I saw the commercial and hoped she would talk to me. We had grown closer over the last six months, and I wanted to be there for her like she had been there for me.

Seeing the look on her face when Rager swam over to her float and leaned in to whisper in her ear, I could tell that I wasn't what she needed. No, my girl looked at Rager like he hung the moon and while I knew I should be worried because she was married to another man, I couldn't help but smile. Jameson and I always believed that Arie should be with Rager. He was one of those guys who when you met him, he fit in perfectly with our family. But Rager was six years older than Arie, and when she was younger, he was always respectful of the age difference. The problem was when it finally wouldn't have mattered, it was too late because she was with Easton.

I cheered for Rager in this scenario, believe it or not.

Lost in those thoughts, I heard my name and strip club mentioned, which naturally drew my attention.

When I looked over to where the guys were all sitting around a cooler filled with beer, I heard Jameson telling everyone how disappointed he was that I wouldn't kiss a stripper during our one and only visit to a strip club together a few months back.

I had never been to a strip club and after my surgery and the installation of my new and improved funbags, a little research was in order. I wanted to see how the new girls measured up against

professionals. Needless to say, Jameson was all for the idea. I think
he had secretly waited for this moment his whole life.

"What are you rambling about over there?" I asked, wanting to
see what story he was feeding the guys.

"I was just telling everyone how I'm just really disappointed
that you wouldn't kiss the stripper giving you a lap dance." Jameson
had a genuine look of disappointment on his face. He had the same
look at the club when I told him there was no way I was going to
make out with some random chick flashing her tits in my face.

"You need to let it go, Jameson." I made my way over to him,
sitting down on his lap. "It's never gonna happen."

Spencer, of course, had to give his two cents. "I don't get your
hesitation. She was hot."

This of course only succeeded to make Alley angry. "If you think
it's so hot, why don't you kiss Tommy?"

Spencer's face went green, and then white. Pure fucking white.
"Why the hell would I do that?"

Hell, even Tommy looked concerned, his sunglasses tipping
down to eye Alley.

"Because why is it okay for you guys to want to see us kissing
another girl, but you can't kiss another guy?"

Spencer shifted in his chair to look at her, I mean really look at
her, like what he was about to say was the most important thing he'd
ever said. Not likely. "Look, babe, me kissing Tommy, that's just
fucking disgusting. No one wants to see that shit. But Sway, kissing
a hot stripper who has her tits in her face, well that's just fucking art.
Guys would line up around the block to pay and see that."

Jameson nodded. "That's what I'm saying!"

I couldn't help but laugh. Spencer had a very specific way of
looking at the world, and I couldn't deny his logic. Nobody wants to

1 6 8

see him kissing Tommy. Hell, I didn't want to see anyone kissing Tommy. Man or woman. Alley, on the other hand, stood up, swaying slightly because as I said, we were all pretty wasted, and smacked Spencer in the back of the head. "You're a fucking pig. You know that?"

Looking up to give Jameson a quick kiss, I noticed the look of disgust on his face. I couldn't help but laugh. "Is me sitting on your lap that disgusting to you?"

Jameson looked down at me, his face scrunched in confusion. "What? No. Why would you ask that?"

"Well, you looked upset."

"I'm not upset with you. I'm disgusted by Dave."

I had to roll my eyes because this was not a new development. Dave brought disgust to most people he met. Mostly because he had weird obsessive-compulsive disorders.

"Why now?"

"Well, have you ever watched him? I mean really watched him?"

"No, why would I do that?" The thought actually made me shudder.

"I've been sitting here watching him, and I have to be honest. I'm severely disturbed by what I'm seeing. Have you ever noticed that he is constantly smelling his fingers?"

"What do you mean smelling his fingers?" I was almost afraid to hear the answer.

"Anytime he touches something, usually one of his body parts, he smells his fingers. So far I've seen him wipe his armpits and sniff his fingers… and just a minute ago he stuck his hands down his pants to scratch his balls, and again, he sniffed his fingers." Reaching up, he ran his fingers through his hair and then stared at me. "I'm thinking there is something seriously wrong with that bastard."

"I don't know why you're so affected by this. He drank gasoline last week. There's always been something wrong with him."

"Good point."

Willie came back, maybe for more abuse, and sat next to us.

Jameson leaned back and stared at Willie's shorts. "Your board shorts look like a cheap motel."

I burst out laughing knowing where he was going with that one. I loved drunk Jameson. Fucking loved him so much.

"Why's that?" He then pulled at the crotch trying to gain some room. They were seriously *that* tight you could see the outline of his dick.

"No ballroom," Jameson noted, looking away.

It took Willie like five minutes to understand the joke, but everyone else got it.

After dinner and giving the grandkids s'mores, I pulled Jameson aside for his birthday present. Me of course.

We were only like a minute into it when Rosa knocked on the door. "I have to pee."

"Fuck off, Rosa. Go away."

She didn't. Naturally. "If I slide my phone under the door, will you take a Snapchat so I can add it to my story?"

Jameson slammed his shoulder into the door, breaking it. "GO. THE. FUCK AWAY!"

"I don't know why you're being so mean," Rosa said to us when we were laying on the ground because my husband just broke the door. "It's not like I haven't watched you two have sex before." And then she snapped a picture of us naked.

"What the hell are you talking about?" Jameson asked her, covering himself with a towel and then ripping her phone out of her hand and put it in the toilet. "When have you ever seen us having sex?"

"Nothing. Never mind. And you're paying for that phone."

Jameson stared at me in disbelief. "I paid for that phone the first time."

CHAPTER FOURTEEN —JAMESON

Pick – Refers to when a car is trying to pass another car, the car under attack may pass closely by the attacking car, such that the attacking car is on the same side of the passing car. The passing car then has to back off and get in line with the lead car in order to pass the slower car.

OCTOBER 2030

KNOW WHAT PISSED me off more than anything?

Bad media. And it seemed between Jack's death and Easton, I had a lot of it. I knew Arie and Easton had problems. I did. And I ignored it for a while, until I couldn't any longer. Not with my daughter pregnant and the appearance of Easton cheating on her.

"Unless you want me to knock those off your goddamn face, I suggest you remove your sunglasses," I warned when Easton walked inside my office at JAR Racing. I mean what kind of fucking idiot did that?

Lately, this idiot.

Surprisingly, he removed them and sat down in front of me.

"What's going on with you?" I was never one to beat around the bush. If I had a problem with you, you fucking knew it, and I had a problem with this. I pointed to the article in Racers Edge indicating Easton was sleeping around with a model.

Easton stared at me, slouched as if I wasn't his fucking boss and signed his damn checks. "Nothing. What are you talking about?"

"Well, I'm talking about your general attitude these days. I've tried to stay out of this, but it's not easy when you're acting like this."

A practiced look of innocence passed over his face, his brow lifting. "I really don't know what you're referring to." Easton stared at me with a blank expression, searching my eyes. Maybe he was trying to see if I was serious, or maybe he was just that stupid. Regardless, the lack of respect Easton showed only pissed me off.

"Let me remind you, of who you are because you've seemed to forget." My voice took on an authority figure, one that if he had any sense, he'd listen to. "I get the lifestyle, the temptation to be that superstar they want you to be, both with the fans and the women that flock to you when you're on top. But you're married to my only daughter. While this is affecting my business and you're pissing me off, you're disrespecting my daughter, and that's where I draw the line."

He didn't say much, just stared at me like I didn't know what he was going through. The truth was, I knew exactly what kind of temptation he had. I nearly lost my marriage over it, and I didn't even act on it. I was simply in the wrong place at the wrong time and had a huge misunderstanding. What was going on with him and this model, it wasn't a misunderstanding. It was him fucking up.

Leaning forward, I placed my elbows on the desk. "Who do you want to be known as?" I asked, keeping my stare level with his. "If you want to be with her, be with her. Don't sneak around behind her back and don't give the press a reason to doubt your intentions." I picked up the magazine and pointed to the model. "Who's this model? Is this something or nothing?"

Arrogance I knew well marred his features as he shifted in his chair, his head skewed slightly toward the door. "Does it matter? And you know how it is."

"No, actually I don't. All I know is you've been seen with her a lot, and it looks bad."

Easton was growing impatient, his tone turning aggravated. "This doesn't have anything to do with my racing, so I don't see how this has anything to do with you."

"See, that's where you're wrong. It does. You race for me. Your image reflects my company." I leveled him a glare, hoping he understood where I was going with it when I said, "You're racing because I chose for you to race. I can take that away at any point."

"I've won you three championships." He snorted, pushing out a deep breath. "And you know, I'm tired of being treated like this." Throwing his hands up in aggravation, they landed with a slap on his thighs. "You've never given me a chance. Nothing I've ever done has ever been good enough for you. I'm not your golden boy," he told me with a confidence I wanted to wipe from his smug face.

I shook my head and glowered at him, my body tensed. How dare he accuse me of not treating him well. "What are you talking about?"

"Rager. I know for a fact he has an indefinite contract."

"First of all, that's none of your business." I couldn't believe he was bringing Rager's contract into this, but then again, I could because Rager's always been competition for him. "And second, I've never asked you to be anyone else. I let you take the lead in your career. When you came to me and wanted to race all three divisions, I never said a word. I gave you a chance. Don't disrespect me. I can take it away just as quickly as I gave it to you. If you want to keep racing for me, don't give me some kind of bitch excuse as to what's going on. It's bullshit."

Easton crossed his arms over his chest, watching me closely. "I don't think this is about my racing at all."

He was smarter than I gave him credit for. This meeting was never about his racing. I knew in my gut Arie wasn't carrying Easton's kid. There was just no way. But I also knew or had a strong suspicion that Easton had not been faithful. I saw him at the track and the way he watched the women around him. I know when another man was stepping out, it was obvious.

"All right, you want to know, fine. You're fucking around on my daughter. I was trying to keep it professional, and you know, it doesn't sit well with me. You have a family on the way."

Easton laughed, shaking his head as he stood. "Come on now, Jameson. We both know there's more to this than me screwing around. Do the math."

Ungrateful asshole.

Of course I did the math.

AS I WAS coming out of the office ten minutes later, I heard the guys fighting, or at least I heard them destroying my fucking shop.

"Fuck... come on, guys." I yanked them apart, holding Rager back with my hand on his chest. "That's enough. You're destroying shit in here."

Rager looked at the floor, clenching his jaw when he saw the engine on the ground and then snapped again, lunging for Easton. Tommy and Willie just stood there, watching and handing money back and forth, no doubt betting on who would win this fight.

"You son of a bitch!" the blistering anger in his voice echoed throughout the shop. "You ever call her a bitch again. I'll make you eat your motherfucking words!"

Bitch?

I stood between them; my shoulders squared up. "What the hell is going on in here?" My head whirled to face Easton, my voice cold. "And *who* did you call a bitch?"

Rager eyed him smugly, straightening out his posture as if he couldn't wait to see where this went. "Go ahead, tell 'em, Hollywood."

"Nothing." Easton spat blood, lifting his shirt to wipe it over his eyebrow. He was bleeding all over the fucking place, so I grabbed a shop towel behind me and handed it to him.

When neither one of them had said anything, I glanced at them, my hands on my hips. "Someone better explain why there's an eighty thousand dollar engine on the ground."

Again, neither one of them bothered to say a goddamn thing. Bending over, Rager picked up Easton's sunglasses, tossing them at his feet. "Now ya gotta reason to hide behind your shades."

Easton said nothing, but I could tell he was bothered by what Rager had just said.

With his palms raised in defeat, Easton gave me one last look as he twisted, picking up his sunglasses. "If you see my wife, tell her I'm looking for her."

So that was what this was about. Arie. *Fucking figures.*

"Get your ass back in here, Rager," I yelled when Rager headed to his truck. After reaching for his hat, he turned and came back inside the shop, his head hung when I asked, "What the fuck was that?"

I couldn't understand how either of them thought I'd be okay with that shit happening in the shop. No fucking way.

This wasn't Rager. Sure, he was just as hotheaded as the next racer, but I could see he still hadn't calmed down either.

Tires screeched in the parking lot as Easton sped out and I nodded to my truck. "Come on, let's go have a beer. We need to talk."

I TOOK RAGER to the restaurant because not only was I hungry, but it was somewhere I could potentially talk to him in private without someone in the shop coming up to us.

Rosa approached the table, a pitcher of water in her hand as she eyed me carefully like she was about to dump it in my lap. Wouldn't have been the first time.

Her gaze turned to Rager and his beat-up appearance. "What the fuck happened to you, killer?"

Rager raised an eyebrow seeming annoyed. "Killer?"

"Did he do this to you?"

"Yeah, I didn't win." Rager slouched to one side, relaxing. "Boss man wasn't happy."

A slow grin formed on my face when Rosa glared at me. "That's child abuse."

"How so? He's twenty-nine."

Rosa reached for the pitcher of beer and I shot her a glare. "You dump that on me like you did last time and I'll have you deported."

"Ha." She started to walk away. "Good luck."

The both of us laughed as Rosa strutted over to the hostess station where she kicked her feet up and put a sign up that read, "Seat yourself."

I tipped my beer in his direction. "What's going on?" He waited for a long moment, thoughts scrambling I was sure. "I expect you to tell me the truth."

"It was just a long time coming," he finally told me.

Nodding, I focused on the stage to our left and the construction workers attempting to finish on time. I knew there was more to their fight, especially for Rager to take a swing at Easton. Sure, Rager would pop off to just about anyone at the track but inside my race shop, a place of business, it wasn't like him. Over the years, the kid had truly earned my respect for his regard for what should and shouldn't be done. This just wasn't like him. Unfortunately, I had to be the boss man and explain what happened would never happen again. "I don't know what's going on with you and Easton, or you and my daughter, but what happened in the shop today will not happen again. It's a place of business. I don't want to see that shit ever again, understand?"

He nodded, sheepishly. "Yes. I'm sorry it happened in there," he was quick to say. "I'll pay for the damages."

"That's not necessary." And then I raised an eyebrow. "But if it happens again, it's coming out of your paycheck." Ordinarily, I wouldn't have handled this situation so well, but given what was happening around me with media and my dealings with my own brother regarding Cole, I saw a different side of this.

After a few minutes, I took a deep breath and rubbed my eyes. "I'm stepping down from Riley-Harris Racing at the end of the season."

Rager studied my face. "Is that what you were talking about with Easton?"

The last person I would have told was Easton. "No... I haven't spoken to anyone about this except Sway." Leaning forward with my elbows on the wood table, my hand jerked through my hair, shaking my head back and forth. I couldn't believe how hard this was to just tell him, think about what it would mean when I told the teams. "It's not something I've taken lightly. But since Jack died, I want to be here with my family, and not there. I want my attention on JAR Racing, where it's always been."

Rager leaned back in the chair crossing his arms over his chest. "What happens with the Cup teams then?"

"I haven't decided yet." I hadn't. I didn't even know who would take over at this point. "It's my name on the line here." I hadn't intended on telling Rager any of this but after today, it just sort of poured out of me. I also knew Rager wouldn't say anything to anyone. He respected me enough to keep this private, I knew that much.

When I made the decision to step down from Riley-Harris Racing, it wasn't easy, but then again, Sway made it easier when she suggested Spencer take over. I just hadn't announced it yet.

With Emma and Spencer owning equal shares in the company along with CST Engines, I still made most of the business decisions because that shit came second nature to me. Neither of them wanted anything to do with CST Engines, so that remained my company.

What I wanted was to step down from everything NASCAR related and hand it all over to Spencer.

CHAPTER FIFTEEN — JAMESON

Fill the mirrors — When a driver is pressuring another driver so feverishly that the rear-view mirror is filled with their pursuer.

SEPTEMBER 2032

MY LIFE HAD once again entered what I referred to as the fast lane. Seasons flew by, my kids had more babies and Sway and I remained the crazy center of all of it hoping we were doing something right.

Arie was now the PR director of JAR Racing and traveling with us full time. With three kids, it was tough on her but she managed to do it just fine. She had more trouble keeping Rager out of hot water with the media than me. Go figure. Never did I think that would happen.

Alley had moved over completely to Riley-Harris Racing along with Spencer, their new owner, and though we didn't see them as much as we used to, it seemed to be a good move for him.

Axel and Lily were doing better. Since Savannah had been born, they seemed closer than ever. Lily traveled with us a lot more when the kids weren't in school, but we never had them in the pits since Jack's accident.

Casten and Hayden, well, they were Casten and Hayden. Up to no good most of the time.

What hadn't changed much was my feud with Aiden and his lawn.

"I want my lawnmower back." Aiden glared daggers at me as we stood in front of the shop loading the trucks before we headed out to the west coast for the final swing of the Outlaw races.

"You know what, Aiden, you're totally right and you know what I'm going to give you?"

"What?"

"Jack shit." I laughed, pushing a tool cart inside the hauler. "Now if you'll excuse me, I have actual work to do instead of mowing lawns."

Aiden and his fucking lawn.

"I knew a guy who got the tip of his finger cut off. He was a real dick," Rager said to Willie, looking over at him when he spilled oil on Rager's white shirt as he pushed the other pit cart.

Willie stared at him, and then me, and then back at Rager, who stood up and glared at him. I had no idea what they were arguing about, but Rager was exceptionally moody. I couldn't blame him. Arie informed us we had a meet and greet to do as soon as we made it to Washington. Both of us hated autograph sessions.

"Are you calling me a dick?" Willie asked, scratching the side of his head.

"What do you think?" Rager grumbled, bumping his shoulder into him.

Willie looked at Casten when Tommy walked away. "Was he really calling me a dick?"

"What's that all about?" I asked Casten, motioning to Rager walking away.

"Arie's pregnant again and being a bitch this morning."

Again? Holy shit. Man, Knox was only what, five months old?

I raised an eyebrow. "She's pregnant again? Jesus, they have like five kids."

Casten laughed. "They have three."

"They have twins, too, though. That's like four babies in one."

"Okay, so that would mean nine kids if your math is accurate, which we all know it's not. You don't even know how old I am."

"Yes, I do. You're what... thirty now?"

"Not even close. I'm twenty-four."

"Oh, right." I gave a nod to Rager. "I should go talk to him."

"Before you go...." Casten held up his phone and mine buzzed with a text from him.

Casten: Cole's in deep.

"Why did you text me?"

He shrugged. "More dramatic this way."

Sighing, I tucked my phone away. "How deep?"

"Nate's looking for him."

Hanging my head, I groaned, scrubbing my hands down my face. What the fuck was wrong with this kid? Cole, Alley, and Spencer's youngest son was constantly in trouble with drugs and borrowing money from a fucking drug dealer.

"Do you know what Nate wants?"

Casten scratched the back of his head. "Not sure. Cole's not answering my texts. Apparently Anna's looking for him too. He knocked her up."

Usually when Cole went silent, we didn't hear from him for months.

"All right." I looked over my shoulder at Alley and Spencer at the other end of the shop, arguing.

Beside me, Rager shoved Willie into the wall when he pinched his ass. "Knock it off!" he yelled at him.

Pulling Rager aside once the trucks were loaded, he chewed on his thumb. "Sorry."

"Don't apologize to me. Sometimes Willie needs to be shoved." And then I caught his worried eyes. "What's up?"

"Just... a bad day." And then he turned to leave, yanking his hood up over his head.

Jesus, and I thought I was moody these days.

"Are you mad Arie's pregnant again?" I asked, following him inside the hauler, refusing to let him get away.

"No... yes, maybe a little. It's just we can't even keep track of the twins and Knox. Now we have another one on the way."

I laughed, leaning into the side of the hauler as he stared at me. "You know how that happens, right?"

"Shut up. Yes, I know *how* it happens. I just fuck," he cursed, pacing now.

"Hey, man. Relax. You guys are great with the kids. It'll be fine."

He snorted, shaking his head as though he didn't believe me. "Yeah, right."

Truth was, I didn't know they would be fine. Four kids were a lot, especially with their lifestyle, but if anyone could make it work, they could. They had love and a relationship a lot like Sway and me, and we did just fine over the years. We lost the kids on a handful of occasions at the races but eventually everyone turned up unharmed.

WHENEVER WE RETURNED to the west coast there was a sense of sadness that followed. Though it would always be my hometown, after Jack died in Cottage Grove, I think it was a reminder of how quickly our lives changed.

It'd been three years since he'd passed and it never, nor would it ever get easier to be in the pits at Cottage Grove, which was where we were tonight surrounded by the majority of our family. That was when Hayden came inside the hauler, pissed at her husband.

Hayden threw a positive pregnancy test right at Casten's head. "I'm going to kill you. You said you got a vasectomy."

Casten looked like he was sweating bullets and picked it up to stare at it. "Hypothetically, yes."

Oh no. This was bad. Sway leaned into my shoulder. "She's really mad at him."

I grinned. "It's great."

She rolled her eyes and continued to watch them argue.

"No." Hayden shook her head. "There's no hypothetical about it."

"Okay... I didn't go through with it." He turned to Rager for support. "He didn't do it either."

"I wasn't scheduled for one," Rager defended from where he sat with Arie on his lap, Bristol sitting on hers. "You were. Though I think I need to go back and get one now."

Arie turned around and slapped his shoulder as if she was offended by that remark. "You said nothing while we were making the baby."

Rager refused to answer her.

"Right." Casten turned back around. "Anyway, I mean, fuck. They were gonna stick a knife near my junk. What was I supposed to do?"

She glared. No. Actually glared wasn't the right word. More like scowled with a murderous expression. "You. Asshole."

He dropped to his knees kissing her belly. "I'm sorry."

"I don't forgive you."

"Well, you will at some point."

She pushed him away. "Not likely."

Casten glanced at us when Hayden was out of sight. "She loves me."

"Yeah, sure."

NOVEMBER 2032

IT WAS LATE and the last place I wanted to be tonight was at the shop getting my car ready for World Finals, but I guessed I should have thought about that before I went and tried to make a pass on the outside last night in Salina. I'd rather have been in bed with Sway.

Pulling my phone out of my pocket, I checked the last message she sent me with a picture of her sitting on the bed waiting for me, proudly displaying her tits. Ever since the surgery, she has been obsessed with them like a fancy new toy five years later. I could understand her excitement. They looked amazing.

"Jameson!" Spencer shouted, slamming the door. "Are you in here?"

Fuck. Spencer found me. "Yep."

There went my quiet night.

Taking a deep breath, I prepared myself as my brother approached me. I wasn't the least bit surprised he showed up. Casten was right, Cole was in trouble when he disappeared. He ended up getting arrested a few months back and me, thinking I could help out when Alley called me in tears, I bailed him out of jail and paid off Nate, his drug dealer. I had my reasoning behind it, but Spencer didn't always see it the way I did. Which was why he stormed inside the shop looking for me.

"It's always about you. You think the fucking world revolves around you, and you can just interfere with everyone. For years I've let you take the lead. When you raced, it was always your neck on the line so I stood back and let you do it your way. Well, guess what, Jameson? This is not one of your goddamn races. This is my family. Stay out of it."

There we were again, arguing about Cole and his stupid-ass decisions but nobody—not even my brother—got away with talking to me like that. Maybe my mother and Sway would too, but even then, they'd better have a good fucking excuse.

What Spencer didn't know was how many times I'd bailed his youngest son out of jail. I wasn't not about to tell him either. Fuck that.

"He was in trouble and he came to me," I felt the need to tell him.

That was essentially a lie. I hated lying to him, but the truth was Alley was the one who called me and asked me to help, but there was no way in hell I was going to tell Spencer that.

Spencer may be pissed, but if he knew Alley came to me for help, I had a feeling he would fucking blow a gasket. Mostly because he told both of us to stay out of it.

Get this, I don't listen very well. Surprised? Probably not.

He leveled me a serious look. "I'm not a fucking idiot. I know what's going on. It's my kid and you need to back the fuck up. For once, this isn't about you," he added. "You can't control *everything*. I told you not to help him anymore."

Did I deserve that? In some ways, I thought I did.

"I mean, fuck, Jameson." Shaking his head, he threw his hands up and began pacing the shop. "When Casten was a kid, he stole cars as a fucking sport." His brow raised. "Did I ever interfere with that? Did I ever tell you how to deal with him or how to punish him? No. I didn't. I stayed out of your kids' lives."

Standing, I buried my hands in the pockets of my jeans. "That's totally different and you know it, Spencer. This wasn't just about me bailing Cole out of jail. He borrowed money from the wrong people. People with connections. If I let him stay there, shit was going to happen. I mean, fuck, man, what was I supposed to do, let them beat the shit out of him and hope he survived?"

Spencer hung his head and then looked back up at me through his dark lashes. It made him look more intimidating that way. Mostly because that was what he was trying to achieve. "You should have come to me."

"And you would have blown up on him and made it worse, or better yet, maybe even ignored it." Shaking my head, my heart pounded as my irritation for the situation amplified. "What the fuck does it matter anyway? It's over and done with, and he's out of trouble. No harm done."

He raised an eyebrow and took a step toward me. I could actually count on one hand the physical arguments Spencer and I had been in. It looked to me like I was about to head on over to the other hand. "No harm done? Are you fucking kidding me? You just can't fucking stay out of it, can you? You just can't leave shit alone."

"I get that you're pissed, but back off," I growled, hoping he understood I wasn't fucking around.

"So you bailed him out." He practically spat the words at me. "And what exactly do you see happening now? You think Cole is just gonna see the err of his ways? Fuck, Jameson. Your money can't fix everything. I get it, you've got money, a lot of fucking money and because of that you think you can just buy your way out of everything."

My jaw clenched at the accusation. I'd never bought my way out of anything. Sure, I had money, more than the rest of my family, but still, I didn't throw it around like it was nothing.

"Don't you come in here and act like I'm the asshole for trying to help. Fuck that."

Naturally, I never backed down to Spencer. I was the younger brother. Older brothers were kind of like meeting a bear on a trail. *Don't make eye contact, but also don't back down. The moment they sense fear is the moment you're done for.*

Spencer raised his hands and for a minute, I thought he was actually going to take a swing at me, but instead, he grabbed the back of his head and paced like a caged animal.

"Jesus Christ, Jameson, how is it that you can be so damn smart but so fucking stupid at the same time? Cole has a big problem. It's bigger than just getting into trouble and having to be bailed out of jail. Why is it you can't see that by you being there to clean up his mess every time he fucks up, he's never going to learn how to fix his own damn life?"

If you asked me, he was overreacting. How could I turn my back on the kid when I knew exactly what those drug dealers were going to do to him if I didn't help? I guessed in some ways I did it because I had hope Cole would turn himself around if he knew there was someone willing to help him get on the right track.

"You know, fuck it! I'm telling you right now, stay out of my business, Jameson. If Cole calls you, tell him no." He waited for me to look at him, his blue eyes stone cold. "I mean it. I find out you're helping him again behind my back, and the next conversation we have is going to be a lot more painful for both of us." Turning around, he took a few steps away from me.

"You're overreacting." Of course I would say that. Would he expect anything different?

He stopped and turned to face me. He knew I had to have the last word. "Am I? What if this was Casten?"

His fist clenched at his side, and I was wise enough to know I needed to say something else. Believe it or not, I'd gotten wiser in my years. "Listen, you've got my back," I told him, attempting to diffuse him. "Always. On the track, in my life, you've been by my side through everything and I'm just trying to have yours."

Spencer snorted, his jaw flexing. "I get it. I'm the comedic relief for this family, but this is where it stops. You don't go behind my back and take care of it. He's *my* kid and *my* problem. Stay out of it."

"Look, Spencer... When I was seventeen, I left home knowing nothing and you were there for me, *always*. You're taking this the wrong way. I'm not trying to do this to one up you. I'm doing this to help you. I will never stand by and watch my family be threatened. I'm sorry. I won't."

"It's not your fucking decision, Jameson." And then he shoved me back against my toolbox. "Don't you think I know what's going on? Alley and I have been dealing with this for the last ten fucking years. It's been tearing us apart. I'm doing this to teach him a lesson he desperately needs to learn. I'm not asking a lot of you, but I'm asking you to back out on this one."

I could see where this was heading. We were about to say something we would regret, and I didn't want that. So I held my hands up. "Okay, I'm out of it."

Did I really believe I was?

No.

STAHL

CHAPTER SIXTEEN — SWAY

Port — The opening in an engine where the valve operates and through which the air-fuel mixture or exhaust passes.

DECEMBER 2032

"**WHAT ARE YOU** making?"

Alley looked at the pot of marshmallows and Rice Krispies. "Oh, dumb question."

"Where's Spencer? "

Tears formed in Alley's eyes. "He's not coming over."

She didn't get a chance to say any more before Jameson came in the room holding two bags of wood chips for the smoker. "Why the fuck not?" He appeared offended, which he probably was and set the bags on the counter. "It's Christmas. He's just being selfish now."

She made a face, probably remembering their argument. "Said we needed some time apart."

"It's fucking stupid," Jameson grumbled.

Leaning into the counter, I poured the Rice Krispies mixture into the pan for the kids. "He found out that Jameson paid off Nate, didn't he?"

Alley nodded.

"I can't believe he's not coming over for Christmas," Jameson interrupted sitting down next to Nancy who was just as shocked that her son wasn't coming over. For as long as Jameson and I had been married, Christmas day was always spent at our house because no one else wanted to fuss over it. "How childish."

"You knew how he felt," I pointed out. "You went behind his back and lied to him about it."

He shot me a glare. "I never lied to him."

"Yes you did," I said, picking up my coffee cup and sitting next to him in the booth next to the kitchen counter. "

"You went behind his back." By the look on my husband's face, I should have shut up right then. Should have. "It's the same thing."

His eyes opened wide with surprise. "You're making a big deal out of it."

"I am not. You're being dumb about this." Like any wife telling their husband they were wrong, I avoided all eye contact and settled on the wood table and the patterns.

He waited until I looked at him and then glared, holding my stare as he lifted a cookie from the plate in front of him and shoved it in his mouth deliberately. "How dare you call me dumb!"

Says the man he shoved a cookie in his mouth during an argument. Nancy found it entertaining and began to laugh. "Oh my God, really? Stop it. I'm trying to help you."

"By calling me dumb?"

"Just listen."

He groaned, tossing his head back. "That's hard for me."

"Everyone knows that by now."

"Not helping."

"You should just call Spencer and apologize."

The mention of his brother's name brought a hint of his former irritation back. "Nope. I have meat to cook."

And then he left. When he was outside, Alley dropped her head into her hands. "He's staying at a motel in town. This is so dumb."

JAMESON KNEW HE was wrong, even if he didn't want to admit it. For that reason, he kept to himself, outside with his prime rib with Rager, Axel, Lane and Casten. With his hands buried deep in his pockets, his head bent forward, I knew he was going over the conversation with him and Spencer. He was like that. Unable to let something go until he'd found an answer.

He once lost the Cup series title by one point to Tate. One point.

The entire off-season, he struggled with it because he knew where he'd lost that one point. It was when his temper got the best of him and he made a move on the inside of turn two. He got into the side of Paul's car and lost two spots. He managed to get one back, but never that second place finish that would have gotten him the championship.

So during the offseason, he couldn't just let that go.

Now with Spencer not coming to Christmas, the statement was clear. Jameson overstepped.

I'd be the first to tell you my husband could be controlling. Not in the ways you'd think either, but he also had a huge heart and Cole was a weakness for him.

He once had this kid working for him. Remember Grady? He gave that kid a chance when he shouldn't have, because he thought it was the right thing to do. Sure that backfired on him, but he gave the kid a chance to do right by him.

"What's going on with him?" Arie asked, carrying a sleeping Knox in her arms as she rubbed his back. When she turned, I noticed his face was covered in frosting, along with Arie's shoulder.

"Knox is the only kid I know that sugar puts him to sleep," I told her, reaching out to rub Knox's back once.

Arie laughed and maneuvered herself to a sitting position, careful of her expanding belly. "I know. I wish it worked for the older two." Giving a nod to her left, I noticed Bristol and Pace running around the family room jumping from one couch to the other with their shirts off. "Really though, why is dad acting all weird today? Is it because of Uncle Spencer?"

"Yeah, Spencer said he wasn't coming and it put him in a bad mood."

Arie thought for a moment, and then shrugged. "He had to know it was going to upset Uncle Spencer when he bailed Cole out again."

"I know." My stare found Jameson again, his posture still rigid and uncomfortable, as though he couldn't let it go. "He knows that too."

Arie winced beside me, her hand on her stomach. "This damn kid is kicking the shit out of me today."

"Did you have sugar today?"

She frowned. "No, but I had caffeine. I'm tired of being pregnant. I mean, honestly, since I had sex with Rager thirty months ago, I couldn't... and I've literally been pregnant for twenty-five of those months." I could tell by her face, she'd given some thought to this. "I'm making him get a vasectomy now."

Rosa walked in. "Is it because he has outlaw super sperm? Or because you can't keep your legs closed?"

Arie glared at her. "You shut up. You're sleeping with Tommy."

Rosa looked over at me, and then Arie. "You're a bitch when you're pregnant, and by your calculation, is all the time, so really, you're just a bitch all around."

Laughing, I touched Arie's shoulder. "At least you're beautiful when you're pregnant."

Wrong thing to say apparently because Arie glared at me. "As opposed to when I'm not?"

"I didn't say that." And then I glanced to Rosa who shrugged, as if to say, told you so.

There was no way to end that conversation well and I was thankful when Hayden came in. With Arie and Hayden pregnant at the same time, they actually balanced one another out well.

"I'm starving. When is Jameson gonna be done with that meat?" Hayden asked, sitting next to Arie. They gave each other a miserable sigh and stared at the plate of cookies that were nearly gone by now, and then their husbands who were responsible for their situation.

"I think you've had enough meat in your life." Rosa eyed Hayden up and down. Leave it to her to piss off the pregnant women in the house in one afternoon.

Hayden refused to acknowledge her, mostly because Gray walked into the room and then right outside to where the guys were to hang on her dad. Gray was a daddy's girl and if Casten wasn't around, she wanted Jameson. Everyone else she pretty much ignored. Even her mother.

"I really hope this little girl likes me." Hayden leaned back in the chair to touch her stomach. "You hear that. You better like me damn it."

As I watched the girls talk about their babies, it reminded me of how Emma, Alley and I used to do this very same thing and now this year, it wasn't the same, yet again. When Jack died there was a void at Christmas, something none of us wanted to acknowledge let alone speak of, and now it seemed that way again, like an unavoidable engine failure. You knew it happened because someone forgot to put the oil plug back in. But no one wanted to take the blame.

SINCE THE KIDS were little, every Christmas night I sat next to the fire in the living room sipping hot chocolate. It was something my mother did when I was younger and I always thought how peaceful that must have been. Once I spent my first Christmas with three screaming toddlers, I knew then she was on to something. Though my kids weren't toddlers anymore, theirs were and I still found pleasure in just sitting next to the fire and enjoying the time alone.

"Sway?" Jameson called out.

Craning my neck forward, I noticed him coming into the family room. "In here!"

I glanced up to see Jameson's eyes were gentle. He'd thought about this a lot today. "I was wrong. Now what?"

I knew what he was referring to. Spencer.

"I'd say call him, but I think you should wait a little while. And you need to apologize in person."

"He's not going to listen to me," Jameson grumbled sitting next to me, the side of his face lit by the flickering of the fireplace.

He might not listen to Jameson, but for him to admit he was wrong was going to take some time and I bet long enough that both of them would have a chance to calm down.

STAHL

CHAPTER SEVENTEEN —JAMESON

Protest – A complaint filed with officials, generally used to check for illegal components, scoring errors, or inappropriate driving techniques.

JUNE 2033

"**WE HAVE A** problem," Alley noted, coming into the back room of the restaurant where I was signing off on Aiden's order forms he had ready for me.

I'd heard that so many times in my life, I didn't even react to it anymore. It was probably something stupid, like a prank gone wrong and maybe someone was missing their hair.

"Oh yeah, what's that?"

Alley's face paled. "It's Cole... and Casten."

"What the hell do you mean, Casten? What happened?"

"Cole apparently went back to using... owed some money to Nate again. Nate showed up at the shop looking for him and Casten apparently told him to get the fuck out. It went from there."

"Is he okay?"

Alley's face crumbled. Tears she fought to hold back streaked down her face. "I'm sorry, Jameson. I don't know." Shaking her head, she paced, her hands shaking at her sides. "Cole said they beat him pretty badly. They had a bat and Casten was knocked unconscious. Cole called 911 as soon as he could and then called me right after. From what he could see, Cole thinks he may have some broken bones."

"Are you fucking kidding me?" I stood, the chair flipping over behind me. "Goddamn him." As I rushed outside to my truck, Alley followed.

"Jameson... there's more...."

More?

My blood ran cold. "What?"

"Nate and his boys took some stuff from the sprint car shop." Her words were rushed, as if she knew she had to get them out before I lost it completely. "Said Cole should consider it payment for the money he owed them."

Turning around to face her, it was all I could do to stand there and listen to this. "What did they take?"

Alley wouldn't make eye contact with me. "They took an engine." I knew there was more. Alley still wasn't looking at me which meant whatever she had to tell me was only going to get worse. "And Jack's helmets."

Goddamn it!

Out of everything in that shop they took, that was the one thing that was irreplaceable. Not because they were worth so much money, but because they were Jack's. His helmet collection was the one thing he loved as much as racing and those fuckers stole them. That did it. My heart stopped and whatever control I had left in me snapped. I became blind to anything but getting to the shop.

Dialing Sway's number, I jumped into my truck to rush over there.

When she answered, I could tell she had been laughing. She had that lightness to her voice and my chest tightened knowing what I was about to tell her was going to rob that moment from her. "Hey, babe. Whose there with you?" I heard voices in the background but I couldn't make out who they were.

"Emma and Arie. Oh wait, Hayden and Gray just walked in. Why? What's up?"

Drawing in a heavy breath, I gripped the wheel tighter as I pulled out of the parking lot of the restaurant. "I need you to have Emma drive you and Hayden to the hospital. I'll meet you there but I need you to head there right now."

"Jameson, why would I go to the hospital?" Her voice trembled with each word. "What's going on? You're scaring me!"

I shook my head trying to clear out the rage. I needed to get back my fucking control so I could explain the situation to her. "Alley came by the office and told me Casten was working at the shop when some guys came in looking for Cole. There was a fight and Casten was hurt. The paramedics are on their way and I need you to go to the hospital so you're there when they arrive. I'm going to the shop."

She gasped. "Oh my God! Do you know how badly he's hurt?"

"No. That's why I need you to go straight to the hospital and be there when they arrive. I don't know what his condition is."

"Okay. We're leaving now." The fear in her voice took over, her words scrambled and inconsistent.

"I'm headed to the shop to see what I can find out," I repeated. "I'll meet you at the hospital as soon as I can."

"Jameson, please promise me you won't do anything reckless."

"I'll see you soon, okay?"

A heavy sigh rang through. She noticed I didn't promise her. I couldn't. "Okay."

Pulling up to the shop, I arrived as the paramedics were loading Casten into the ambulance. I could tell he was still unconscious, maybe, but I wasn't able to get to him before they slammed the doors.

Rushing to the door, I noticed Tommy standing over to the side talking to Rager. Taking a step toward Tommy, he watched me carefully, waiting to see what my reaction would be.

"Where's Cole?"

Reaching up, his scratched the back of his head. "He's cleaning up in the shop."

As I turned to find him, Tommy stepped in front of me to block me, his jaw tightening. "Jameson, maybe you should take a minute to calm down."

"Get the fuck out of my way."

Our eyes met I knew he could see it, the rage taking over. For once he made the right decision and stepped to the side holding up his hands. Even Rager didn't stop me.

Storming inside, I couldn't fucking believe this shit. The place was trashed. Equipment and parts were strewn all over the place and there was blood on the floor that I could only assume belonged to Casten.

My son. My shop. My *motherfucking* shop. It wasn't even the shop that pissed me off. It was *what* was stolen from me. I mean, yes, I was upset about Casten. I was. They beat my son to the point where his blood was painting the floor and he was being taken to the hospital. But the fact that they stole Jack's helmets and beat Casten was what really set me off.

Cole held up his hands when he saw me coming, dropping the broom to the concrete floor. "I can fix this!"

"The fuck you can!" I took him by the shirt; my hands fisted in the fabric so tightly it ripped at the edges. "How are you going fix this? Huh? You can't fix anything, you fucking crackhead! All you do is fuck shit up." I picked him up and threw him roughly against the wall. "What the fuck is wrong with you?" In a moment, I'd forgotten my own strength and fisted my hands in Cole's shirt taking a firm hold of him. Slamming him back into the wall once more, I was right in his face spitting anger.

He was so ashamed that he wouldn't even look at me. He sputtered out some words, unable to make a clear defense or formulate an excuse.

I slammed him back again. This time I heard his head make contact with the wall. "You're a worthless piece of shit! I gave you so many fucking chances to turn your life around, and this is how you repay me?"

"Don't you think I know that?" Tears stung his eyes, never spilling over, but the emotion welled up before he dropped his gaze to the floor scattered with blood. "I don't know... I don't know what to do anymore...." And then he broke down, his chest shaking. "I tried. I just can't stop."

Seeing him sobbing wasn't easy, but it wasn't easy seeing my son's blood at my feet and knowing my grandson's possessions were taken either. My instinct was to fix the problem, but Spencer was right. I couldn't. I just couldn't. Not this time. At some point, I had to give up and let him destroy himself. If I didn't, it'd destroy our family, what was left of it.

"How did you even get in that deep again?" I let go of him, expecting an answer.

"Fuck, Jameson. I don't even know." He raised an eyebrow, the corners of his mouth turning downward in regret. "One minute I'm doing good, and the next I'm at a party lookin' for a fix."

"That's your excuse? You don't know?" I had to turn away. I couldn't look at him and not want to kill him.

As I turned, Cole grabbed my arm. "Jameson. I'm sorry. I'm so fucking sorry."

"You're sorry?" Raising my eyebrow, I smiled and reached for a valve cover on the bench and tossed it across the shop in anger. "YOU'RE FUCKING SORRY?" the question roared out of me and then followed by the crashing sound of the valve cover hitting the wall. "How fucking sorry are you, Cole?" I screamed until my voice broke apart. "Are you so sorry that you could look Jack in the eye if he was here and tell him you're sorry his most prized possessions were stolen but you couldn't help yourself again? Do you think he would be okay with that? And what about Casten? He's not just your family, Cole, he's you're only fucking friend, and now what? He's being taken to the hospital with fuck knows what injuries. You and I both know there's a chance he won't be able to finish the rest of the season when he was leading the points. What about him, huh? You gonna tell him how fucking sorry you are, you son of a bitch!"

Rager came inside the shop having heard the noise. "Jameson," he warned when I shoved Cole again, his body going limp against the floor. He wasn't putting up a fight because he knew damn well he'd burned this bridge once and for all.

With what seemed like pent-up frustration, I paced the floor as I heard the shop doors open, my hands in my hair, tugging to find a reason behind this. "How many more times are you going to fuck up?"

Cole didn't answer, shaking his head as tears fell freely. It only made my anger soar higher. How dare he sit there like some victim crying over something he did. It was his bullshit that caused this.

I was in his face again, my body shaking with an anger I might never be able to tame.

"How many more times? You've destroyed your parents' marriage... put your best friend in the hospital... left your pregnant girlfriend... now what? Who's left Cole? I'll tell you who? No one! There's *no one* left to help you."

Something in him changed as my words washed over him and his own self-pity took over. Angry with me now, a side of him I hadn't seen in a while, he spat through gritted teeth and tight lips, "I said I was sorry, Jameson! What do you want me to say?"

"Don't you get it, Cole? It doesn't fucking matter what you say to me. I'm done." Running the back of my hand over my jaw, I knelt beside him, my breath on his face. "So do me a favor, don't say you're fucking sorry when we all know you don't mean it."

Cole stared at me, his breathing heavy, unable to formulate a response.

His voice broke like the glass beneath my feet. "And I am sorry. I never meant for any of this happen and I never wanted to bring Casten into this."

"But it did happen didn't it? And you did bring Casten into it." He interrupted me again—apologizing once more—but I raised my voice. "Enough Cole. I've said it and I mean it. I'm done. I will never help you again. Ever. And you're done here at JAR Racing."

He nodded again, his face void of color, the consequences of his actions clear in his bloodshot eyes. "I know."

I hated this. As much as I wanted to, I'd never be able to fix Cole's problems. Ever. The more Alley and I tried to fix it, the worse it got. There was nothing left to say; at least, I didn't feel there was. Turning, I faced Rager and Axel, who'd watched this all unfold.

"Make sure he leaves and turns in his key."

Rager nodded, his hands buried in his pockets.

"Can I go by the hospital and check on him?" Cole asked.

I stopped but didn't turn around. "Stay away from Casten. I don't want you within a mile of him, Cole."

I left the shop that afternoon and went straight to the hospital.

Sway, Emma, Alley, Hayden, and Gray all looked up at me with differing expressions.

Noticing me, Sway rushed up to me with tears in her eyes, her finger going straight for my chest. "I told you! I told you to stay out of it and let Spencer deal with it! But you wouldn't listen. No, you knew best. Well, are you happy now?" She scowled at me, her eyes squinting and her tiny nose scrunching in anger. "Casten is somewhere in this hospital with God knows what injuries because your pride always wins out."

She's blaming me for this?

I knew I shouldn't be surprised by this reaction. Casten was Sway's baby and they always had a close relationship. Not knowing what his condition was, whether he was okay or not, was probably killing her. But how was she gonna blame me for this shit? I didn't beat him up.

Unfortunately, she was right. Cole may have been the one to bring this on us, but I had to take responsibility for some of this shit too.

Sway repeatedly asked me to step aside and let Spencer and Alley deal with Cole but I wouldn't listen. I was sure each time I bailed him out or sent him to rehab it would be the time I fixed the problem. But the truth was, all I did was enable him to continue to make the same mistakes over and over. I never held him responsible for what he was doing. Instead, I just decided I knew best and handled the situation as I saw fit. And now here we were and I fucking hated she was right.

After her outburst, Sway pushed away from me and took a seat next to Hayden and Gray. Hayden hadn't said anything to me directly, but I could tell she shared Sway's opinion. When she looked at me, I could see the fear in her eyes and anger.

I sat down next to Sway leaning over with my elbows resting on my thighs. All of a sudden I was exhausted. The adrenaline from my anger had subsided and the weight of what happened began to seep in.

When the doctor finally came in to talk to us, he explained Casten had been beaten with a bat and taken a blow to the head causing him to lose consciousness and have a slight concussion. His leg was broken in four places and would require surgery to insert pins to help stabilize the bones. And his arm was broken as well along with a few ribs. One of the broken ribs resulted in him suffering a punctured lung. As if the leg wasn't enough, a punctured lung was a season-ending injury in itself. He was going to need months of rehab to recover.

"We've moved him to a room up in the ICU and you can see him shortly," the doctor told Hayden. "We'll schedule surgery in a couple of days once the swelling has gone down."

Hayden drew in a steady breath, her arm around Gray at her feet. "Thank you."

I breathed a sigh of relief knowing he was going to be okay, but it still didn't ease that gnawing sense of disappointment in myself that this happened.

HOURS LATER WHEN the girls went to the restaurant to get Casten barbecue because he refused to eat hospital food, I was able to talk to him alone. The room filled with anxiety. It wasn't like I hadn't seen one of my children in a hospital bed. Over the years there had been more times than I cared to admit where I found myself sitting next to one of my kid's hospital beds making sure they were okay. Usually it was after Axel or Casten wrecked on the track, or when Arie had given birth. This was different though. I couldn't help but feel responsible for Casten being here and it was fucking killing me.

Casten slowly turned his head, wincing at the movement, and opened his eyes to stare at me. I stared back. It was obvious he was struggling to think clearly in spite of his condition, to find a way to make sense of it. As I searched for words, Casten did the same.

"Casten, I am so sorry that this happened." I told him before he could say anything.

Casten's expression turned to confusion as he reached for his water beside the bed. "This isn't your fault, Dad. Why would you be sorry?"

Standing, I moved his table a little closer to his bed side and then took a seat again. "I made it possible for this to happen. Even after everyone told me to back off, I kept bailing Cole out. Giving him the opportunity to keep making the same mistakes over and over."

Nodding, he knew what I was feeling was somewhat warranted. "Speaking of Cole, where is he? Is he okay?"

"Don't know. Don't care."

The worry in his eyes was evident. After everything that happened to land him in this hospital bed, he was still concerned for Cole. His brow creased for a moment, then smoothed as his eyes took on a knowing look. I couldn't believe it. He'd already forgiven his cousin.

I stared at my hands, flexing my fists. How could he forgive him? How?

I blinked, astonished. "How can you forgive him so easily?" I mumbled, my heart racing.

"He's family, Dad."

"But he nearly got you killed," I pointed out.

"It doesn't change anything. Yeah, this fucking sucks ass"—he shook his head, wincing with pain at the simple action, seeming to struggle with the thought—"and I'm out for the season but he's my cousin. He has no one else."

I glared. "I appreciate your loyalty, Casten, but you need to stay away from him."

"Well, I certainly will be distancing myself, but I'm not holding this against him."

"Yeah, well, I'm not so forgiving."

"Cole's an addict, Dad. He's got an illness and it's not something he can always control. Addiction is a selfish beast and yeah, Cole has definitely caused a lot of shit because of it, but I'm not going to turn my back on him. I'll never stop caring."

I couldn't help but smile. This was Casten. He always saw the good through the bad. Even when Axel punched him a couple years back, he never once turned his back on his brother. He internalized and put himself in Axel's shoes having lost his son. It seemed he was doing the same for Cole now.

"You seemed to have gotten pretty smart in your twenty-five years."

He smiled. "You got my age right."

My anger began to disappear but when I saw the look of pain cross his face when he laughed, it reminded me I wasn't so forgiving.

WHEN I FINALLY left Casten's room, he'd finished eating and was half asleep with Gray and Ryder in his arms watching a movie with them. Heading down the hallway, I noticed Alley talking to Sway and Hayden in the waiting room.

Once I entered the room and closed the door behind me, they stopped talking and turned to me. Alley had tears in her eyes with a look of true devastation. "Jameson, I am so sorry. I never would have thought this could happen. I really thought he was doing better."

I knew I had to put my anger aside. It wasn't Alley's fault this happened. As mad as I was about what had gone down, the truth was Alley had been dealing with the hurt and fear that came with Cole's addiction for years. Hell, it was what was driving her and Spencer apart. I understood her guilt because I shared it, but I also needed to reassure her that she didn't need to be sorry. Not for this.

"There was no way you could've known this was going to happen," I told her, putting my arm around her shoulder. "Cole had us all fooled and no one person is to blame. You and me, we had an equal hand trying to help him time and time again. You're no more to blame for this than I am."

When I let go of Alley, Sway came toward me taking my hand and giving it a reassuring squeeze. Her expression had softened and I could see she was beginning to calm down.

In the distance, I noticed Spencer walking down the hall and within sight.

"How's Casten?"

Watching my brother, seeing the genuine concern in his face, the guilt returned.

Spencer warned me to stay out of it. He asked me to leave Cole to pay for his mistakes but I didn't listen. I didn't give my brother the respect he deserved. I didn't allow him to handle his family his way. Honestly, Spencer had always been the one to have my back whether he agreed with me or not. I couldn't help but feel like shit when push came to shove, I didn't do the same for him.

Walking up to him, I placed my hand on his shoulder. "Hey, can you come with me for a minute? I want to talk to you."

He nodded, watching Alley's reaction and her tears. "Yeah, sure."

We walked out of the waiting room and down the hall. Once we were out of earshot of everyone, I turned to him. I couldn't help but smile a little. He looked so much like Jimi that it made me think that if my dad were still alive, he would have called me an asshole a long time ago. And I would have agreed with him.

"Look, Spencer, I'm sorry. Okay. And I don't say that very often so I hope you understand it's coming from my heart when I say I overstepped here. You asked me to back off and I didn't listen." My shoulders raised and then dropped with a heavy breath. "You were right. Nothing we did was going to fix Cole. I should have given you the respect to handle your own family. I'm sorry."

I didn't know what to expect. Spencer had been so pissed at me for going behind his back. I almost expected him to throw an "I told you so" at me but instead, he just smiled and pulled me in for a hug.

"Thank you. I appreciate you apologizing." And then he drew back, leveling an amused look at me. "I know that was hard for you."

I stared at him in confusion. "That's it? You're not mad?"

"Fuck yeah, I'm mad, but what good does it do for me to yell and scream? Your son is lying in a hospital bed right now because of Cole. I think my point was made that we should have stopped helping Cole a while ago. I'm just sorry Casten's hurt."

I dropped my stare to the ground. "He's out for the season. They beat him with a baseball bat. Broke his arm and a few ribs. They're gonna have to put pins in his leg to stabilize it. It's gonna take months for him to recover."

Spencer placed his hand on my shoulder trying to comfort me. "I wish I knew where to find Nate, but I don't. Even Cole doesn't."

"Fuck, Spencer, how the hell did this happen?" I groaned, pacing the hallway. "How did I let this happen?"

Spencer leaned back against the wall, his arms crossed over his burly chest. "Jameson, you can't blame yourself for this. Yeah, you bailed him out but it was Cole who made the choice to get involved with Nate again. This is what I was afraid of but now that it's happened, we have to figure out a way to move past it."

I wasn't sure what else to say so I nodded and we headed back toward the waiting room.

Once we returned, Spencer made his way to Alley and took her into his arms. It was the smallest gesture, his arms wrapping around his wife, but it was exactly what Alley needed. She sank against his chest and began to cry. With Spencer holding her, protecting her, she could finally deal with all the emotions since Cole had called her.

As soon as she collected herself, she looked up to Spencer. "What are we going to do?"

Spencer brushed her tears away with his thumb, cupping her face. "It's already done."

A look of panic clouded her eyes. "Wait, what do you mean it's already done?"

"He's on a plane to Washington as we speak. Logan called Van after he heard what happened. Van called me and suggested that Cole come up and stay with them for a while to get him out of town and away from the shit that's going down. He's going to give him a job at the track and see about getting him some help."

I wasn't exactly pleased with what I was hearing, mostly because I owned that track and I no longer wanted Cole working for me, but if he was out of my sight, maybe this could work.

"So you just sent him away? Without even telling me?" You could tell it annoyed Alley Spencer didn't consult her, but then again, did she have anything to argue about on that one? Nope.

"Yeah, I did," Spencer told her, taking a step back. "And I don't really see what there was to talk about. Cole needs help and he needs help away from here where he's constantly being sucked back into that life. Nothing good comes from bailing him out and giving him more opportunity to fuck up. Van has experience dealing with these problems. He has friends who can help. It's the right thing to do."

Standing there watching Spencer take control was something I didn't see very often. For so many years he was happy to let Alley or I take the lead. Seeing him handle such a fucked-up situation with such confidence made me want to punch myself for not listening to him sooner.

Spencer was right. If this had been Casten, I would have lost my fucking mind if someone went against my instructions. I was man enough to admit that.

CHAPTER EIGHTEEN —JAMESON

Retaining Road – In drag racing, a road which leads from shutdown area back to the pits or staging lanes.

FEBRUARY 2034

THE ATMOSPHERE AROUND the shop and the track was different these days. Now that Arie was the PR Director for JAR Racing, she traveled with us, which meant the kids came too. If I thought it was stressful having my kids at the track, it was way worse with the grandkids. Especially after what happened with Jack.

I found myself constantly on alert, watching them and in turn, it was affecting my racing. At some point, we had to make sure the kids were safe. That left us making the decision that the little kids weren't allowed in the pits anymore. It just made sense. Arie, Axel, and Casten completely understood the decision.

What else changed was Cole wasn't around. I meant it when I said he was done at JAR Racing. I wasn't going back on my word.

Spencer sent him to live with Andrea and Van. Van gave him a job at the track, despite my warnings not to. I wanted to see Cole turn his life around—I did—but he burned that bridge with me and it would never be repaired completely.

It was early February when I was at JAR Racing, Casten and I looking over his car for the following week as we were set to leave for Florida for Speedweeks. He had made a full recovery from his injuries, and looking at him, you'd never know a bunch of thugs had taken a baseball bat to him to prove a lesson to someone else. That wasn't Casten. He never let anyone keep him down for long.

"There's a package here for you."

Looking over my shoulder, I noticed Rager standing at the door. "For me?"

He picked up Knox off the floor when he tripped over the torsions bars for the third time that morning. I swear to God that kid was like a bobble head. Constantly falling. "Yeah."

"It better not be a dick in a box." I laughed, walking toward the door where the boxes were lined up along the wall. It was more than one box; it was about twenty of them.

"What's all this?" I asked, glancing to Rager for an answer.

He shrugged, trying to control Knox who was now squirming and crying in his arms. "No idea."

Staring down at the boxes, I picked up the first one that said one of twenty and saw it was from Cole. There was a note inside the box that said: *I know my apology means nothing, but hopefully this helps. - Cole*

Opening the boxes, I smiled. He'd got back every helmet from Nate.

Casten came inside the showroom. "Are those the helmets?"

"Yeah," was all I managed to say, tears constricted my words. Not because he returned the helmets, though I was proud, it was because the helmets were a reminder Jack was gone.

Just as we had the last helmet back in the display case, Spencer came inside dressed in a suit and tie.

Casten laughed, breaking down the boxes. "Where'd you come from, the club?"

Spencer smiled at Casten, his hands in the pockets of his dark slacks. "Easton's wedding."

"He married that Jessie girl, didn't he?" I asked, knowing he did. I heard Tommy talking about it a few months back when Easton proposed to her in victory lane. I think he stole that scene from me.

Spencer nodded and I wasn't at all surprised Easton didn't invite me to his wedding. Why would he? He cheated on my daughter and then ruined any credibility he had with me by lying about it and acting like dick-douche.

"Cole?" Spencer asked with a tilt of his head toward the display case.

My throat tightened again. "Yeah."

When I stared down at the last helmet Jack wore, the tears welled. "Have you heard from Cole lately?" I was trying to change the subject, anything to stop from crying right now.

"Yeah. I flew out with Alley and Anna so he could see the baby."

I'd forgotten Cole was a father now. A son, Austin, about two months old.

"He seemed good." Spencer reached up and loosened his tie, his weight shifting to one side. "He was excited to see us."

Casten raised an eyebrow but smiled. He'd wanted to know Cole was doing better too.

"Think he's using again?" I asked when Casten took the boxes outside to the dumpster.

Spencer drew in a deep breath. "I doubt it. Van's drug testing him every two weeks and he lives with them so I'd think he'd know. He's been working a lot, marketing mostly."

"Yeah, I approved the commercial for their season opener he did the other day. He's still got it." Truth was, Cole was incredibly talented when it came to photography and making videos, and if he kept it together, he could do great things. I wasn't sure I'd ever hire him back with JAR Racing, but from a distance, I was okay with him working for me again.

"Wanna go get some lunch?" Spencer asked, nodding outside. "Lane's at the restaurant with Axel. Thought we could meet them over there."

A rush of emotion crept in again when I gave the helmets one last look. "Yeah, I'd like that."

CHAPTER NINETEEN —SWAY

Loud Pedal – Refers to the accelerator, gas pedal or throttle.

AUGUST 2034

I COULDN'T BELIEVE how quickly our lives changed. It was as if I blinked and I had three kids and eleven grandkids. Crazy thought.

Casten and Hayden added a little one. A beautiful brown-hair little girl, Rowyn, who was just the sweetest thing ever. Nothing like her sassy older sister, Gray, and rowdy brother, Ryder. Talk about three completely different kids.

And poor Arie, she had her fourth and last baby. Rager was fixed before Hudson was even born. It was a good thing too because the kid was a shit head. He'd just turned one in March and I was positive all that sugar Arie ate had made him mean. Deep down I loved him because he was blood, but I would never babysit him. Arie was on her own with that one. I mean, he broke my nose two months earlier throwing a baseball at my head. No "hey, catch this." Nothing. Just bam, take a baseball to your head. And get this, he loved Jameson. Thought he was the greatest person on the face of the planet. Naturally Jameson was the only one he'd listen to. He'd give Hudson a look and the kid obeyed. It was magic.

Maybe we were crazy, okay, we probably were but after the last couple of years, we decided a family reunion would be fun. Sure, none of us were actually from Hawaii but it was one of the few places no one had been arrested or kicked out of so we decided to go there.

Charlie used to tell me it was important to spend time with your entire family. I remember him talking about us traveling to family reunions as a child, but I was too young to remember them. It got me thinking since Jack died, we hadn't all been together other than Jameson's birthday party on the lake and holidays, but even then, everyone wasn't always able to make it.

The challenge was getting all the schedules to line up but we managed to get a time in August we could all go. Too bad it was hot as a devil's ball-sack there and enough humidity, I believed, to suffocate someone.

We, and when I say we, I meant me, decided it would be fun for everyone to travel together which meant we were forced to fly commercial because our plane wouldn't fit that many people. As it was, we nearly filled the commercial flight with all forty of us. It was like traveling with a professional sports team. A professional sports team whose members were either drunk, fighting, or having sex in one of the bathrooms.

"Who said this was going to be a good idea?" Jameson asked, leaning into me as he watched his brother and Alley sneak into a bathroom together. It was so good to see them back together again. Tipping his head my direction, he gave a nod to the bathroom. "Should we go next?"

"Gross. I'm not having sex with you in a bathroom after your brother has. No way. And I said this was a good idea."

"Fine. I'm getting drunk then." He managed to flag the flight attendant down and ordered a Jack n' Coke. "Go light on the Coke. It's going to be a long day."

The friendly flight attendant smiled at my husband and glared at me.

Jameson eyed me again, raising an eyebrow. "She doesn't like you very much."

"That's because she knows she doesn't have a chance and *I'm* the reason why."

Naturally Jameson smiled at this revelation. "Well, since I'm such a hot commodity, you may want to rethink your refusal to visit the bathroom with me. I'm just saying."

"Yeah." I snorted, turning toward the window and picking up a magazine. "I'll get right on that."

Jameson laughed but didn't bring it up again. He knew better than to think I would ever have sex in any room right after Spencer and Alley. I'd known them too long and they were into some seriously weird shit. Think whips, chains and peanut butter. Enough said.

Once we landed in Kona, it became a waiting game for the luggage. Happened every damn time and someone always lost their luggage. This time it seemed to be Tommy who couldn't find his bags.

I really couldn't understand the problem. I mean aside from us, there weren't that many people on the flight so how could have they have lost it?

As we stood around trying not to completely lose our shit, I could hear Arie next to me rooting around in her purse like she was looking for something.

Arie groaned, her purse falling off her shoulder as Rager stared curiously at her holding Bristol on her hip. "I can't find my phone and there's a hot dog in my purse. That tells me Willie is around."

Rager rolled his eyes at Arie trying to keep a hold on their crying daughter who wanted down to run around in the airport with the rest of the kids. Bristol had a tendency to run away though so Arie knew putting her down wasn't safe.

"Willie," she yelled after him as he sat on the edge of the luggage racks. "I swear to God, if you took a bunch of selfies of your dick with my phone, I'm going to shove this hot dog up your stupid ass!"

Rager groaned, tossing his head back. "Why the fuck did you let him have your purse?"

Willie was known to be slightly obsessed with taking dick pics. None of us understood why either. It was like he had to keep reminding himself he had one. If you asked Tommy or Dave, it was because he was divorced. They blamed everything on his divorce and he blamed them for actually causing it.

"What makes you think I have your phone?" Willie actually had the nerve to look hurt by the accusation. Never mind the fact he was wearing cutoff shorts and a tank top that read: The Man, which pointed to him, and The Legend, which pointed to his junk.

He stole it from Casten.

"Well let's see, if memory serves me correctly, when we boarded the plane you had a hot dog in your hand. And now I have a hot dog in my purse. Doesn't take a genius to figure it out." Arie handed Bristol to Rager and then her bag as if she were preparing for a fight with Willie.

He stood, holding his hands up in defense when she cracked her neck. "Okay, so let's say the hot dog you found in your purse is mine, and let's also say maybe I borrowed your phone to take a picture of my dick to compare to said hot dog. How many pictures count as a bunch which would then lead to you shoving said hot dog up my ass?"

Arie appeared as if she was about to explode. Her face turned red, her shoulders tensed. "Damn it, *Willie*, you have your own phone. Why are you using mine to take pictures of your dick? And why are you measuring your dick to a hot dog?"

Rager, Casten, and Lane found this apparently hilarious and were practically falling over in their laughter.

"Well, my phone storage is full," he explained, as if that would make perfect sense. "Apparently, I have reached my dick pic limit on it so I borrowed yours because the guy at the hot dog stand told me I was buying a foot long, but I had my doubts."

"You know what, forget it. I don't want to hear anything else that comes out of your mouth right now. Keep the damn phone." She turned around to face Rager, who now had tears in his eyes. "There is no way I'm touching anything that was near your disgusting dick." She slapped Rager on the shoulder. "And stop your damn laughing."

"Okay, now you're just being rude," Willie noted, placing his hands on his hips as if that of all things offended him finally. "There is nothing disgusting about my dick."

Arie turned, refusing to acknowledge anything else he said, walking away.

Willie watched her, a smile creeping over his lips. "Hey, Arie, can I get my hot dog back?"

She flipped him off and threw the hotdog inside the men's bathroom she passed by.

An hour later they finally found everyone's luggage. Well almost everyone. Tommy's luggage was still lost which I found amusing because Tommy's luggage consisted of a cooler with wheels that he duck taped shut and used as a suitcase. You'd think that would stand out. Which it probably had. They more than likely thought it was some kind of bomb. Until they opened it.

The airline assured us as soon as they found Tommy's cooler/suitcase, they would send it to our house, so we headed outside to the rental cars.

THE MADNESS CERTAINLY didn't stop once we were at the house we rented. In fact, I think it got worse. Mostly because the guys raced there and two of the six rental cars needed new tires.

Once we were at the rental house and settled the sleeping arrangements, Alley, Hayden, Rosa, Arie and I headed to the store to stock up on groceries and lots of alcohol.

I loved the thought of us all being together, but I was also realistic enough to know if this vacation was going to work, we needed alcohol and lots of it. And as far as I was concerned, there was nothing wrong with being drunk most of the day.

As we gathered up snacks for outside by the pool, Rosa came into the kitchen holding Hudson out to Rager who took him from her. She had offered to change his diaper because no else wanted to. And I was pretty sure she found out why no one wanted to.

"Why are you making that face?" Rager asked, smiling at Rosa. He knew exactly what happened.

"I was changing his diaper and he peed in my mouth!" Rosa gagged, reaching for a towel on the counter and glaring at Hudson who was staring at her like, what the fuck is your problem, lady. It was the look he gave pretty much everyone.

Holding Hudson away from her, Rager bumped Rosa's shoulder with his own, winking at her. "Let's face it, Rosa. That's not the first time that's happened to you."

Rosa gawked at him, just for a second and then shrugged. "No, it wasn't."

After putting away all of the groceries and stocking the refrigerators, we decided we should reward ourselves with some margaritas on the deck. Rosa was definitely for that plan. She needed to wash her mouth out.

Once outside, the guys were out there attempting to push each other into the pool. They looked like a bunch of kindergarteners shoving each other on the playground, but it was amusing to watch.

Lily and Axel were teaching Savannah how to swim. Brody and Lexi were even here for a couple days. Nowhere close to Spencer, but here. I found it a bit sad Cole couldn't make it, but I heard he was at least doing better these days.

"Papa!" Pace screeched when Jameson picked him up over his head, his tiny three-year-old body flailing around. "No swim!"

And of course Jameson threw him in the water. He was that guy, the one all the kids feared around the pool because he thought everyone should get in the water.

Pace was about the cutest kid I'd ever seen. I love all my children and grandchildren but Pace was the cutest. Maybe it was the olive skin, thick wavy black hair and blue eyes, but he just had everyone wrapped around his finger.

When Pace popped up out of the water, his bright eyes reflected off the water as he glared at his grandpa. Pushing his hair out of his eyes, he swam away from Jameson toward the stairs and then sat there with his arms crossed over his chest. "No fair!"

Jameson looked back at me and smiled. "Guess he didn't want to swim."

I couldn't help but smile. This was what I was hoping for. All of us gathered together just enjoying each other's company.

That was until Rosa asked, staring at her phone, "What's a sexy way to say suck your balls?"

Arie gawked at her, practically spitting out her drink and sat forward in the lounge chair. "Rosa! Gross!"

"What? You can't tell me you haven't sucked on the bad boy's balls, Arie." Rosa stirred her drink with her finger and set her phone down. "Don't be so prudish. You forgot, I heard you two making Hudson."

That shut Arie up.

Rosa leaned forward, her hands resting on her thighs. "No, seriously, how would you say suck your balls, but in a sexy way?"

All the girls stared at one another waiting for someone to say something. Only we couldn't because none of us could think of a sexy way to say it. Believe it or not, I hadn't said "suck your balls" to Jameson. Sure, I'd had them in my mouth a time or two, who wouldn't... but to actually say it seemed weird. But this was also Rosa we were talking about.

Finally Hayden speaks up. "How about suckle your frenulum?"

"Suckle your frenulum?" Contemplatively, Rosa tapped her index finger to her chin. "That's not balls?"

"No." Hayden brought her margarita to her lips, shrugging. "But it's all connected so I think it would get the point across."

"You're right. I'm gonna go over there and tell Tommy I'm going to suckle his frenulum tonight."

I wish I could blame the conversation on our being drunk but this was just how we were.

Hayden watched her get up and walk over to them, say what she needed and then she returned, strutting confidently back, seeming satisfied with herself as Jameson shook his head, having heard what she told Tommy.

"How'd it go?" Hayden asked when she sat back down.

Straightening out her dress like she was suddenly a lady, Rosa crossed her legs. "Very well, actually, but I think Jay thought I was telling him that, so it got awkward really quickly."

Hours later, nobody had moved. The only people who seemed to have any energy after the long flight were the kids playing in the pool.

Eventually I had moved to Jameson's lap as he sat in the lounge chair with me, a beer in one hand, the other on my thigh as Zac Brown blared through the air.

Beside us, Casten and Hayden did rock, paper, scissors to see who got to get shitfaced between them.

Hayden won, which was why she was now standing on top of the table doing what she interpreted to be a hula dance yelling, "Don Ho is dead! I'm the head ho now!"

Whatever that meant.

Casten stood close to her in case he needed to catch her, but while he waited for the inevitable fall, he was laughing his ass off recording the whole thing. Those two were meant for each other. Looking at them, you'd think they were two carefree kids, not parents of three children under eight.

"If you die with an erection, does it stay that way?" Tommy asked Jameson, catching both of our attention.

I turned to Jameson, curious his thoughts on the subject. I never thought about it but as drunk as I was, it seemed like a reasonable question.

Jameson contemplated that for a moment and stared with a sense of seriousness at Tommy. "I suppose if you're Edward Cullen you do."

Emma arrived with another round of margaritas and handed me one and then stared at Jameson's chest and stomach.

"What are you looking at?" he barked, reaching for a margarita.

"You just...." Her voice trailed off and that only pissed her brother off more.

"*What*, Emma?"

"You're muscular."

He raised an eyebrow, a smile forming now as he flexed his stomach. "Oh please. I've always been this way."

"I know, but you're old now. I thought gravity would catch up with you."

"Well, it didn't." Jameson seemed pleased by this and stared at me. "*See*... even she says I look good." And then his voice took on a seductive tone. "Why don't you come upstairs and show me some love."

"Nah... I really want to try surfing with the boys." I gestured to the beach where Rager had the younger boys out there teaching them how to surf.

He groaned and watched Jacen, Sawyer, and Jonah wading in the water. "Why do we always have to plan activities? Why can't we just go on vacation and I don't know, relax, have sex and eat good food?"

I ignored his comments all together and asked, "Do you remember Tour Guide Ted?"

"Is he here?" Jameson looked panicked, his eyes darting around the beach. "If so, we're leaving!"

"That was Costa Rica. We're in Hawaii."

"So what? He could have been deported."

I stared at him blankly only to have him roll his eyes. "Shut up."

THE NEXT DAY, everyone hit the beach after breakfast. The nice thing about the house was the private beach so we didn't have to worry about anyone offending the locals. This was by design, believe me. Been there, made that mistake before.

That was a blessing considering Tommy's bags still hadn't arrived. Tommy, being the problem solver he was, came down to the beach with a towel wearing one of Rosa's bikini bottoms.

Not okay. I didn't care what he thought; it didn't look like he was wearing a speedo. There were bits and pieces falling out of all ends.

"My eyes burn," I told Jameson, covering them.

He chuckled. "I've seen him naked a lot over the years. I'm blind to it."

Thankfully, Tommy lay down on his towel and passed out still drunk from the previous night so I didn't have to watch him run down the beach or anything.

"We gotta get him some clothes," Jameson noted, slinging his towel over his shoulder and looking the other direction.

"Agreed," Arie grumbled, hauling two of her four kids behind her, their tiny feet moving quickly to keep up with her as they giggled.

The kids were having a great time playing in the sand and splashing in the water. It seemed like everyone was enjoying themselves and I was so grateful that we were able to have this, again, I couldn't help the emotion surfacing. Or maybe it was that the day we arrived in paradise, shark week started and I was flooded with all those girly emotions that came with that week.

Jameson noticed my tears. "Hey, you all right?"

Turning, I faced him and then buried my head against his chest. "Yes. Thank you for agreeing on this vacation."

Reaching up, he rubbed my back and then stopped immediately when he noticed I had tanning lotion on. God forbid he get it on his hands, right? Right. "If you're having such a good time, why are you crying?"

I avoided his stare. "I'm not crying I'm just... look at everyone." I motioned around with a wave of my hand. "They're so happy."

He lifted his chin in a nod. "What about you, are you happy?" I couldn't miss the curiosity in his tone when he looked me in the eyes.

"Of course I am."

"Does that mean we can go back to the room and have sex?"

"No."

"Damn it. Fine. I'm going surfing."

"There're sharks in the water," I pointed out, waiting by the towel I had laid out in the white warm sand next to me.

Jameson turned immediately and sat next to me. "Good point."

BY THREE, EVERYONE was starting to get cranky and hungry so we headed back up to the house.

Nancy had volunteered to stay back with the babies so they could take their afternoon naps while we enjoyed the beach. We found her on the deck reading, with the baby monitor set up next to her.

"Hey." She smiled, noticing us all. "Did everyone enjoy the beach?"

Jameson kissed her on the cheek. "Yeah, it's beautiful. You need to go down there and check it out. But not with Bill. Unless you plan on pushing him in." He flopped down in the chair next to her, working on the label of the beer in his hand. "Why did he come here anyway? He's not family."

Nancy and I both shook our heads at him and his reasoning for anything related to Bill, Nancy's friend. "Well, neither is Rosa, Tommy, and Willie, yet they're here."

Jameson rolled his eyes, uninterested in anything else besides trying to find a way to off Bill. "Whatever."

Tommy walked up still looking like shit. "Why did you guys let me fall asleep? You know how sensitive my skin is. Fuck." He cringed, moving gently onto the deck. "Now I'm gonna be all red."

"We let you sleep because the alternative was you walking around in that banana hammock," I told him, handing him another towel and hoping like hell he covered up his junk. "Nobody wants to see that shit."

Spencer sat down next to his mom and Jameson. The look on his face told me he was up to no good. "Hey, Tommy. Did you enjoy your nap?"

Nancy giggled when Tommy turned around and she saw his back. "I see Spencer still has his drawing skills." And then she tipped her head to the side. "What's the top part? It looks like a waterfall coming out of the top." And then the realization hit her and her cheeks turned about as red as Tommy's back. "Oh. Spencer," she scolded. "That's gross."

"No. I did not enjoy my nap." Tommy clipped, trying to see his back. "Now I'm gonna peel. Stupid fucking beach."

When he turned and we saw what Nancy was referring to, we finally understood the look on Spencer's face.

Spencer once drew a floor-to-ceiling dick on a hotel wall. He repeated this art on Tommy's back with sunscreen, only he made it look like there was cum spurting out of it.

Sitting back in the chair, Spencer puffed out his chest a little with pride and smiled before tucking his hands behind his head. "It's a work of art my friends. It's amazing what you can do with a little sunscreen and a lot of time."

Tommy disappeared into the house to see what his back looked like as Rager glanced at him, and then did a double take of his back and burst out laughing.

Casten took a handful of raisins, chewing slowly. "They taste like chocolate."

Hayden smiled and set Ryder on the floor. He took off outside to the pool where Jameson was throwing kids in. "Ryder likes chocolate covered raisins, but not the raisins."

It took Casten a minute before he understood what that meant. And then he spat them back in the bowl, pushing it to the middle of the table.

Tommy came inside in only his underwear. Apparently, Hawaiian weather was too much for him. I was thankful they were at least black underwear this time.

"I'm starving," he announced, scratching his balls. It made it worse he was wearing white underwear. "I thought we were going to a Luau or something."

"For the love of Christ I hope they find his bag soon," Hayden whispered to me and then smiled at Tommy. "Have some raisins." She handed him the bowl.

"Thanks." Wrapping his arm around her, he popped a handful in his mouth. "I knew you'd like me eventually."

She eyed him offensively, and then stared at her foot, the one bitten by a snake seven some years ago. "Yeah, sure."

When she left, Tommy leaned into my side. "She spit on these, didn't she?"

"What do you think?"

His head hung. "I think she did."

"**IS THAT A** dick on his back?" Brody leaned forward watching Tommy take a seat next to Jameson, his shirt off because he said even the slightest fabric against his skin hurt. He was asked twice to put on a shirt because of his dick sunscreen drawing. Both times he spat on the people who asked, like he was a fucking camel or something. It'd be a miracle if he wasn't arrested within the hour.

"Yep." Spencer goaded with pride.

"Well, fuck my ass."

Jameson, Spencer and I stared at Brody. For being such a talented driver in NASCAR, he said some really stupid shit sometimes. Spencer shook his head like he was disgusted with his son-in-law. He probably was.

"I wouldn't say that too loud around here." Willie hushed Brody when a group of men walked by.

"Why?"

"Because we're in a foreign country."

"Hawaii's not foreign," Jameson noted, like he knew what he was talking about. This coming from the guy who thought Rio was next to China. "It's part of the United States."

"Why are we doing a family reunion here anyway?" Casten flopped down in the chair next to me. "None of us are from here."

"Rosa might be." I gave a nod to her on the stage trying to hula dance. She couldn't. Not even the slightest. She looked like a cat trying to walk with shoes on.

"What are we waiting for? I thought we came here to eat?" Casten asked just before downing his third beer of the night. Apparently, his raisins weren't enough earlier and he was starving.

"The pig. They're digging it up." Axel gave a nod to where they were in fact digging a pig from the ground.

Savannah, who was on Axel's lap, threw her head back in a screaming fit and nailed Axel right in the jaw. He immediately handed her off to Lily, his face red with anger. That was like the fourth time she'd done that tonight. Poor Savannah could never get it together at the dinner table, or any other time. She was by far the crankiest kid I'd ever seen. Nothing made her happy unless it was Jonah making silly faces at her. Word to the wise, never let her and Hudson play together.

"This is a fucking joke. I'm starving." Casten growled and then looked at Willie who was using a razor blade to cut a hole in a coconut. Or trying to. "Where did you get a razor blade?"

"From my sock." He shrugged placing the razor blade back in his sock. "Security is a fucking joke at this place."

"Why would you even need a razor blade?"

"It is the amazon."

Casten sighed. "No, it's not. It's fucking Hawaii."

"Oh, right. Well still, what if a pig chases me?"

I pointed to the pig roasting in front of us. "Yeah, cause he looks terrifying."

Willie turned to me. "I'm not eating that."

Once the food arrived, everyone seemed to calm down a bit and unfortunately, drank as much as they ate, including Jameson and me. I don't know what my deal was but the drinks were delicious and I had no self-control.

Then the fire dancing started. Their first mistake was allowing Jameson, who was shitfaced, to dance with fire.

"What's your name?" the girl wearing a grass skirt and a coconut bikini asked, her long black hair draped casually over her perfect olive skin. She was fucking beautiful. If I were ever going to consider a threesome, it would be with Kelly, the Hawaiian fire-dancing beauty.

I was also sure it crossed Jameson's drunk mind when he leaned into her and said, "Whatever you want it to be."

I could count the number of times I had seen my husband drunk enough that he flirted with other women. Certainly confident enough not to worry, I found it entirely too entertaining and burst out giggling at the table.

"I haven't seen Jameson this drunk in a long time." Emma snorted and grabbed Hudson—Rager and Arie's youngest—before he waddled up to the fire. He was fascinated with anything that had flames. Believe me, he had the makings of a pyro.

"It's awesome!" Tommy shouted, whooping and hollering beside us.

"Don't give him fire!" I yelled, practically standing on the table.

They didn't listen to me, and Jameson ultimately caught poor Kelly's skirt on fire. And fuck me if she wasn't hotter naked.

"I'd do her," Hayden whispered, looking at me in disbelief, her eyes wide. "Fuck, how is her skin that perfect?"

My concern grew when Jameson nearly dumped his alcoholic drink on her to put the fire out. At least he was trying to help, but still, not the brightest move. "I think it's something in the air here. They all have pretty skin."

Emma frowned and reached for her drink. "Jameson looks ridiculous up there. It's like Grandpa Ken dancing next to Hawaiian Barbie."

Emma was just jealous because she wanted to dance on stage.

It was about twenty minutes after my husband caught the girl on fire, and she had since changed, when a boy, just as beautiful as her, approached me to dance.

"Ah, well that's sweet of you, Island Boy, but I'm a grandma now. I can't be dancing with boys in high school."

I wasn't sure he understood what that meant. Actually, I was positive he didn't because the next thing I knew, Island Boy was teaching me how to hula dance.

You know what, I was way better than anyone else at it too. Maybe because I was drunk and my own dancing ability seemed superb to me, or it was that I was just that drunk that I didn't care.

Either way, it was a blast. And I had no idea how it happened—goes back to being drunk—but I ended up showing Island Boy the funbags before the night was out.

It was then my drunk husband had something to say. "What the fuck, Sway?" He growled, grabbing me by the arm and covering my chest with his shirt.

"Whatever. You were dancing with the Hawaiian beauty over there. How come I can't?"

He looked offended, his mouth opening and shutting a few times before he said, "She sure as hell didn't see my dick, now, did she?"

"Well, I didn't show island boy my crankcase. I showed him the funbags." I motioned around me, drink still in hand and splashed poor island boy in the face with it. "I just wanted to see if they compared to the girls around here."

"They look better to me," Island Boy popped off with, his dark hair swept from his beautiful face as my drink dripped from his perfectly chiseled jaw. He looked like a tan Greek god statue.

Jameson shoved him back away, and into Tommy who squealed like the pig they buried and ate, because we hit his sensitive skin. "No one asked you."

"She asked me." Get this, Island Boy stood up to Rowdy Riley.

I was very interested to see where it would go when Jameson stared at the kid with a look I hadn't seen in a while. "What the fuck did you just say to me?"

"I said... she *wanted* me to see them," Island Boy smarted off, focusing again on Jameson.

"There will be no version of this where you're gonna walk away, so stay out of it." Jameson stepped closer, his movement both guarded and a warning. He was one, drunk, and two, Island Boy could be some kind of UFC fighter or something. He never knew.

A familiar standoff, one I'd seen many times, began between Jameson and Island Boy. One where I knew Rowdy Riley might make a return any minute.

Jameson's eyes swept over his, gauging a reaction he knew he'd have. "Why don't you go back to showing these other woman a good time and leave mine alone?"

Island Boy looked at his buddies gathering around, all of them showing amusement. "I think you're—"

Jameson smiled a cold, bitter smile, letting out a venomous, cynical laugh. "You really think I give a goddamn what you think?" he asked, his jaw tightened. I put my hand on his shoulder, surprised how quickly his temper was getting out of control.

"No, I don't think you care. All you tourists are the same. Come here lookin' for a good time and when you get it, you're good, right? What about her? She's just lookin' for a good time too and she's a little drunk. Who fuckin' cares, man. Relax. You were dancing with my wife and I didn't say anything."

Jameson said nothing. Absolutely nothing.

See, I knew Island Boy and Hawaiian Barbie were married.

Damn, think about how beautiful their kids would be. Like little chocolate kisses of sweetness. While I daydreamed about their pretty babies, Jameson finally loosened up a bit when Hawaiian Barbie came over. "What's going on over here?"

"Your boy's looking at my wife's tits," Jameson told her before anyone else could speak. It was just like him to get the first and last word in.

She laughed, her arm around Jameson. "Oh relax." She then put her arm around her husband. "Eamon's harmless." She extended her arm to me, which I took and dropped Jameson's shirt. So she met me and the enhanced funbags all at once. "I'm Kahlua. But almost everyone calls me Kelly."

"I love Kahlua in my coffee," Casten said, wrapping his arm around my shoulder, before he noticed I wasn't wearing a shirt any longer but only covering myself with Jameson's shirt. Naturally my son didn't look but discretely removed his arm and became best friends with Eamon.

Thankfully they all walked away, and Jameson made me put my shirt back on. "I can't believe you showed him your tits. Stop doing that."

I blew off his harshness and kissed his sunburnt cheeks. "You're cute when you're mad."

"Can we go fuck now? I'm tired of this Luau shit."

Raising an eyebrow, I walked with him onto the beach, hand in hand. "Is that because Kahlua back there got your engine temp up?"

"She may have put a little heat in the engine, sure..." I loved how relaxed he was, his eyes drooping shut slowly, "but I prefer to get racey with someone who knows how to lay on the loud pedal."

I burst out laughing while he tripped in the sand and sat down, chuckling to himself at his ability to turn anything into car jargon.

Leave it to the girl in me to ask, "Did she really turn you on? You never talk about that kind of thing with me." I'm married and understood just because a man had a ring on his finger, it didn't make him blind to the opposite sex. Jameson and I just didn't talk about that kind of thing.

He did that thing where he blinked, maybe deciding if he should tell me the truth or not. "What?"

"Never mind." Despite me trying not to, my cheeks heated. He knew what that meant.

He groaned. "Come on, don't be like that. Was she hot? Yeah. Did I want to fuck her? No. I want you." I still wasn't buying it so he pulled me on his lap to straddle him. "Do you remember that night in Charlotte?"

"How could I forget that?"

He drew back, his eyes searching mine. "Well, my point is it had been like a year since I had sex."

"So...."

"I wasn't having sex because I wanted my best friend." He raised his hips so I could feel his erection through his shorts. I shivered despite the warm humid air, goose bumps moving over my skin. His lips brushed against my neck once again. "And I still want her, always."

Okay, he had a way of making things better.

"I bet you I can make you remember why you chose me, too."

He ground his hips into mine as his lips pressed to my bare shoulder and then he kissed me slowly leaving wet kisses over my skin until his lips found my neck. "I bet you could."

"It's been a while since I did any micro polishing." My finger traced the line of his ready camshaft through his shorts.

His hands moved to behind his head as he lay back in the sand. "Let's see what you got. Don't get any sand on me though."

Lowering myself down his body, his eyes lit up when I had his shorts undone. They rolled back when I went to work, and squeezed tight. His legs stiffened, and he squirmed a little when he met his rev limit.

When I finished, I was a tad breathless and crawling up him. "Did you forget all about Kelly?"

Jameson chuckled, slightly breathless as well. I felt pretty good about my efforts and wanted to remind Hawaiian Barbie I could get the job done in record time.

"Do you believe me now?" His arms reached out to pull me close to him, holding me tightly against his chest. He was quiet for a while before he whispered into my hair, "You will always be what I need."

"**WHERE WERE YOU** last night?" I asked my son who looked like Mardi Gras took a shit on him.

Casten groaned sitting down at the bar outside where Hayden and I were making Bloody Mary's. "What a mess. I said I'd go out with them for a drink. Next thing I know I'm half naked, the bar is chanting my name, and I'm dancing on tables with that Kelly chick from the luau and her husband. I can't do anything in moderation."

"You married Tommy? Do you even love him?" Arie asked as she and Rosa stepped outside to the bar. Almost everyone else was still sleeping, including Tommy who was facedown on the pool deck drooling.

Casten and I whipped our heads around to stare at them as they sat at the bar too.

"Well," Rosa contemplated for a minute and then took a slow drink of her Bloody Mary I handed her. "I think about him when I masturbate so I guess that's love, right?"

"No, not really," Casten told her setting Gray down beside me and then taking a seat next to Rosa at the bar. "I used to masturbate to pictures of Megan Fox, and I never loved her."

Gray stared at Casten, blinking slowly. "What's masturbating?"

Casten looked at me and then Hayden, who punched his ear. "Really, dude?"

He ignored her and looked over his shoulder at Tommy, now awake, groaning about his sunburn. "Maybe that's why he got married. The sunburn went to his head."

"So why *did* you marry him?" Hayden wanted to know. Hell, we all wanted to know.

Rosa shrugged, staring at her candy pop ring. "Let's face it, at the end of the day, he's the face I want to sit on."

Leaning into my shoulder, Hayden whispered in my ear, "Twenty bucks says they get it annulled when we get home."

"I don't know." I took the empty cups from the bar and washed them out. "I think they might actually work. I mean, they've been together for a long time."

"Yeah, but when has Tommy been faithful to her? Him and his orange hair get more ass than a toilet seat sometimes."

"Right? I've never understood it. Maybe because he's Tommy to us."

"Or maybe he's just really gifted in bed," Rosa added, peeking over our shoulders and handing me her empty cup.

"Well, there's that." Hayden cringed. "But excuse me while I vomit."

"What are they talking about?" Jameson asked, no shirt on and scratching his head. I stared, naturally, at his body as he sat down next to Hayden, who he kicked off the stool next to him so he could put his feet up.

She took her new drink I gave her and dumped it on his head.

He stared at her in complete disbelief that she would one, do that, and shock because it was cold.

"Tommy and Rosa got married," I blurted out, hoping to distract him from killing Hayden. He had that look in his eyes.

His brow scrunched as he took a towel from the bar and wiped his face off. "Why?"

"Rosa wants to sit on his face." Hayden smiled, trying to make Jameson uncomfortable. Ever since Jameson began playing practical jokes on Hayden, it had been her mission to get him back. Poor girl would be trying a lifetime but she was good at making him uncomfortable.

Glaring at his daughter-in-law, he stood and took two steps toward her, wrapped his arms around her and jumped in the pool with the both of them.

This was turning out to be a great vacation.

CHAPTER TWENTY —JAMESON

Stressed member – Term used for a method of construction, seen mainly in open wheel cars, where the engine, rather than being supported by the chassis, is part of the chassis.

"YOU'RE SUCH AN asshole." Hayden reached for her towel on the side of the bar.

"Whatever. You poured you're drink on me. How's that fair?"

"Just is."

Gray walked by, looked at me and then back down at the screen pointing to the racing game on her iPad. "I beat your high score."

I ripped the iPad from her hands and yanked her on my lap to sit with me on the lounge chair on the deck.

She glared when she noticed her clothes getting wet. "Gross. Is that sweat?"

"No. I'm wet. Now let's see this game. Who says you beat me?"

"The game."

Staring at the screen, her name blinked at me, mine under hers. "You cheated."

She gave me an offended look over her shoulder. "Whatever. I'm good at it. Once I'm racing in the Outlaws, people are gonna be like, Jameson who?"

Hayden approached us. "Don't be corrupting my daughter."

Gray laughed and dropped her eyes to the iPad, uninterested in anything but the game again. "Pretty sure you and Dad did that years ago."

Being seven, Gray thought she knew everything. I blamed Hayden for it.

"You ready to go?" Aiden asked, coming outside with Spencer wearing board shorts and socks with sandals. Him and his fucking socks.

"For what?" Leaning back in the chair, Gray got up and went about her game, so I kicked up my legs like I wasn't going anywhere when Sway handed me a drink.

Aiden rolled his eyes, like he couldn't believe I'd forgotten what we were doing today. "Fishing."

"I don't want to go fishing."

Sway threw a towel at my face. "No one asked if you wanted to go, but you are. Now get up."

As I stood in the driveway, I came to one conclusion, besides the fact that Sway forced me to go fishing so she could go shopping without me. My family was like a three-year-old hugging a kitten. They didn't know the difference between hugging and suffocation. And that suffocation to me was being on a boat in the middle of the ocean, fishing with them.

Rager sighed beside me when we were getting in the truck to leave. "Think they'd know if we bailed?"

My voice was dejected when I said, "Probably."

Guess who was the fisherman taking us out into the Pacific?

Yep. Eamon from the Luau last night. He still didn't like me and I wouldn't have helped him if he went overboard.

"How long have you and Irish Cream been married?" Willie asked Eamon as they sat baiting hooks.

Eamon gave him this look that was something similar to, I think this dude is mentally challenged. But he answered with, "*Kelly* and I have been married for three years."

Willie nodded, seeming interested. "Kids?"

"Girl." Eamon was short with all his answers, which I found entertaining. Most people were with Willie because you just wanted him to stop talking.

Willie let out a laugh, seeming to find his own thoughts entertaining. "Did you name her Cream?" Twisting, he slapped me on the shoulder. "Get it, Kahlua and Cream?"

I did get it. Didn't mean I found it funny.

Eamon stared at me, his face void of emotion. "No wonder you're an asshole. Your family is weird."

"That's funny. He's the fishing guide too," Aiden remarked, standing beside me as Eamon explained what we were fishing for in the middle of the ocean.

"No, it's not funny." I think there was a reason as to why Aiden always wore socks. He had the ugliest fucking feet ever. "Why is your middle toe flipping me off?"

"Fuck you," Aiden grumbled, reaching for his wet socks. "I'm never taking my socks off around you again."

"Thank God." I grabbed my beer I'd stashed in my bag. I didn't care about fishing, but I cared about beer today. "No one should have to see that bullshit."

Aiden shoved my shoulder practically throwing me off the boat and into Rager, who was behind me. "You're an asshole."

"I know."

I heard a splash behind me and then realized I'd knocked Rager into the water.

"Hey, can I dump this in?" Willie asked, and then proceeded to dump the fish guts and blood into the water, right on Rager.

There were a few problems with that. I mean, we were in Hawaii and we were there to fish. But there were also sharks in the water.

"Willie, you fucker. Help me get back on the boat!"

"You know, you're a real jerk when you want to be."

"I'm in the water with fish blood and guts all over me. I think I get to be more than a jerk."

Naturally, with blood in the water, a shark became Rager's best friend. Why wouldn't it, right?

"Don't panic," Eamon ordered, tossing Rager a flotation ring from the boat as he scrambled around trying to control the situation.

"Panic?" Rager gasped, shaking water from his face as he tried to swim away from the shark, but further from the boat. "There's a motherfucking shark in the water with me. How can I not panic?"

I felt horrible, and then worried about myself. Arie would kill me if a shark ate her husband. Thankfully it wasn't a big shark. More like Jaw's infant son. If he had one. I was pretty sure even if it bit him, we'd at least be able to sew the pieces back on.

"Yeah, don't panic."

Rager shot me a glare, struggling to stay afloat. "You get in here then, Jameson. Don't tell me not to fucking panic."

"Nah." I leaned over the boat for a better look at the shark. "I'll pass."

"What if it bites off his dick?" Willie asked, watching the shark swarm near him. "I bet then Arie might consider me. I mean, like as a last resort."

"The fuck she will!" Rager yelled from the water.

It happened quickly and Rager was actually kind of badass about it when the shark tasted his calf. It was just a nibble if you asked me. He kicked the fucker in the head and I have no idea how, but he jumped out of the water and toward the boat. It was like he had super powers.

Once he was on the boat, leg bleeding all over the place, he scowled at me. "I can't believe you pushed me in."

I pointed to my chest, offended. "I did no such thing. Aiden did."

We, as in me and Rager, decided fishing was over after that and we headed back to shore.

Rager reached for a bottle of rum he'd stashed on the boat. "This vacation fucking sucks."

"Oh don't be so dramatic. It's only because Jameson tossed you overboard." Casten handed him a towel to wrap his leg up with.

I glared at my son. "I did not."

As we walked back to the truck, Rager limping with a bottle of rum, and me and Spencer helping him walk, a girl in the parking lot caught Willie's attention by flashing her tits at him.

Willie watched the hooker closely. "Maybe I should go talk to her."

"Don't even think about it." Casten grabbed him by the shirt, yanking him toward the truck. "I'm pretty sure if she sneezed, her tampon would fall out."

His eyes went wide. "What does that mean?"

"It's like traveling with children," Casten noted and then turned to Willie. "It means she's loose."

"Oh."

He still didn't understand.

"**WHAT HAPPENED TO** you?" Arie asked when we were back at the house, staring at Rager's bleeding leg.

"Shark attacked me," Rager grumbled, tossing himself on the couch dramatically. Knox walked over to him, his hand on his dad's shoulder, bending down to examine his leg. At two years old, he still didn't talk much, but he did rub his dad's head like he understood what was going on with him. And then he proceeded to show him his elbow where he crashed on the pavement earlier today. Sympathy sharing, I supposed.

Rager leaned forward, ruffling his thick black hair and kissed his scrapped elbow.

"It wasn't a full-blown attack," Willie explained, sitting down on the edge of the couch beside Rager. "The shark just took a little nibble because this fucker kicked him in the head."

Rager lifted his good leg and knocked Willie off the couch. "Fuck you. It was an attack." Sitting up, he gestured to his leg. "I need fucking stitches."

Arie examined it, as did Sway. "No, you don't need stitches, but we should clean it."

Rager's eyes met mine and he glared. "Oh, don't worry about that. My kind father-in-law did that for me by dumping a half a bottle of vodka on it. Pretty sure it's fuckin' clean now."

I lifted my hands. "Hey, I was only trying to help. I was bitten by a shark once."

"Sure you were." Rager flopped back on the couch, his arms over his head. "Someone hand me a beer."

Jonah, who thought the blood was awesome, poked at his leg. "Does it hurt?"

Rager glared at Jonah like he wanted to punch a child. "It does when you poke it. Stop touching me."

With Arie sitting beside him, he noticed her bright red leg. "What happened to her?" I whispered to Sway, smiling at Arie and Rager and thinking to myself they were exactly like Sway and me.

"Just wait." She pointed to Casten, who came inside with Rowyn on one leg and Ryder on the other, Gray trailing close behind with an iPad in her hands, barely aware of anything around her. "This is going to be good."

Rager noticed Arie's leg, too, and Casten's grin when he asked, "What's that smell, Arie?"

You would have thought someone lit my daughter on fire with rage. "Fuck you, Casten. Fuck. You."

"What's that all about?" Rager asked, still staring at her leg. "You kinda smell funny."

"I was stung by a jellyfish and Casten straight up pissed on my leg."

Gray snorted and high-fived Casten. "Nice, Dad." And then walked out of the room.

Arie scowled at Gray. "See if I ever take you shopping again, Gray!"

Gray did nothing but flip her hand up, blowing Arie off, her wild mess of brown hair tangled in the wind as she walked out to the pool.

Rager turned his attention to Casten, who sat across from them. "I wouldn't sit so close to her," Rager warned.

Too late. Arie lunged for her brother, tackling him to the ground to rub her piss-soaked leg on his face. "How does it smell now?"

And this is why she's my daughter.

AFTER THE SHARK and jellyfish incident, I think everyone was ready to relax for our last night in Hawaii. After dinner, we took a walk on the beach just before sunset.

"Do you think either of them will go in the water again?" Sway asked, sitting next to me in the sand with another beer she handed me.

"Probably not." As I watched everyone, I smiled seeing Spencer and Alley, hand and hand on the beach. I glared at my mother walking with Bill and then focused on my kids.

Axel had Savannah on his shoulders, swinging his only daughter around with Jonah, and Jacen tried to keep up with Gray on the sand carts. That girl, Gray, no one could catch her. At seven now, she'd beat every record I ever made in quarter midgets. Impressed the hell out of me in a car because she was so damn little, but there wasn't anything she couldn't do in a race car for sure.

Casten was nearby, proudly watching and holding Rowyn, their newest little one, away from the sand because the damn kid wouldn't keep it out of her mouth.

Ryder ran up to me, hugged me and then took off back to his cousins, Pace, and Bristol. Funny enough, out of all the grandkids, Ryder was the most affectionate. He would cuddle with just about anyone.

"Can you believe all these people are here because I got laid?"

Sway raised an eyebrow. "Maybe you should stand up and say that."

"I'm just saying." Leaning back in the sand, I rested most of my weight on my right elbow. "They should really thank me. They're literally here because of me."

"Okay, well"—she leaned back in the sand with me—"let's say hypothetically I didn't play a role in any of that... despite my crankcase remembering it, anyhow, what are you saying, that your balls did good?"

I laughed, remembering Jack's theory on getting a girl pregnant, as did Sway. "Yep. My balls did good." Shifting in the sand, I nodded south between my legs. "They created a family."

Sway rolled toward me, laughing. "This conversation is getting weird."

"Well, you played a role in there too." Kissing the top of her head, I let my lips linger there for a moment. "None of this would have been possible without you."

Sway thought about that for a minute, then smiled at our hands joined in the sand.

"It's a beautiful life we have, honey."

Leaning in, she pressed her lips to mine. "It is."

THE END.

OUTTAKES FROM PACE LAPS

GAUGE – SPENCER

Gauge – An instrument, usually mounted on the dashboard, used to monitor engine conditions such as fuel pressure, oil pressure and temperature, water pressure and temperature, and RPMs.

NOVEMBER 2032

I KNEW ALLEY was enabling Cole. She'd been doing it for years. What I never expected was my own brother going behind my back to help him out after I specifically told him not to.

They purposely went behind my back to protect him again. I wasn't having it. Not anymore. If this was the way they were going to act, I was done with them.

For the first time in my life, I considered walking away from my family. Not because I wasn't man enough to take care of them, but because I was trying to and Jameson constantly found it in my best interest to go behind my back to protect my son. Didn't they realize what they were doing to him?

I mean, I was his fucking father for shit's sake. I knew what was best for him even if he didn't.

Slamming the door to my truck shut, I stormed inside the house barely able to keep myself from shaking. The moment I entered the house, Alley was of course on the phone. "I need to talk to you."

She held up her finger to me.

Nope. Not happening. This wouldn't wait any longer.

Taking the phone from her, I slammed it down, glaring at her. "I need to talk to you right now."

She looked at me with disbelief. "Spencer! That was the president of NASCAR."

"I don't care. We need to talk."

She went to my brother after I asked her not to. And the only reason I knew that was because Cole slipped and told me they helped him.

Crazy as it was—when I found out—it was as if she had cheated on me. I knew she hadn't but the betrayal was there and fucking ugly.

The moment our eyes met, I realized I needed to calm down. No way did I want to come in and talk to my wife like this, but she had to know I would have this reaction. It should be my wife and me making this decision about Cole, not her and my fucking brother.

"Whatever you need to say could have waited, Spencer."

"Yeah, I suppose it would because I don't matter, do I?"

Alley's head jerked back in horror, my words slapping her face. "What the hell are you talking about?"

If she didn't know…. *Fuck that shit. She knows!*

Taking her cell phone off the counter, I sent it flying toward the wall. Her brow scrunched at the sound it made hitting the wall, the screen shattering and echoing through the kitchen.

"What is your problem?"

"My problem?" Admittedly, I never treated my wife like this. I was raised better than to do that, but I was at my breaking point.

"Yes, your problem."

"Funny you should ask that." Leaning into the counter, I crossed my arms defiantly over my chest. "I had a talk with Jameson today. Actually, I'd call it more of an argument."

"What'd you do to piss him off this time?"

"It's nothing I did. It's what the two of you did."

Her expression was one of curiosity. "Spencer, I don't have time for this today."

"Okay, so you don't have time for us. Got it." And then I began to walk away.

Her arm caught mine just before I passed her. "What is it that I did?"

Swallowing over the adrenaline pulsing through me, I stared at her, hoping my glare spoke for my irritation. "You went behind my back and asked Jameson to bail Cole out of jail. That night, the one you told me nothing was wrong, you went behind my back when I told you not to. I'm done. I'm fucking done with this bullshit."

"How did you find out?"

I laughed, bitterly. "Cole told me."

"Spencer...." Alley sighed, attempting to block me from leaving with her hands on my chest. "Calm down. I only went to him because I knew you wouldn't help. I couldn't let our son be hurt by those men. I can't believe you were willing to turn your back on our son."

"Calm down? I wouldn't have to calm down if you would have came to me that night and not Jameson. And I can't believe you did this. You went behind my back to my fucking brother! My brother! I mean, fuck, Alley, you might as well have sucked his dick with how this feels to me."

"Okay, now you're being dramatic."

"You've thought about it, haven't you?" I knew I was being juvenile, but I was fucking pissed.

That pissed her off. "Fuck you, Spencer. You know goddamn well I *wouldn't*."

"I didn't ask if you would. I asked if you've thought about it."

"No. Never."

"And you know, I can't tell if you're lying because I don't know you anymore." Shaking my head, I watched helplessly as tears streamed down her face. "For years I've sat back and let you take the lead on parenting Cole. I let you take the lead in every part of this relationship because it's who you are. You take control and I love that about you, but this... I can't fucking do this with you anymore. I specifically told you not to help him. I fucking begged you to stay out of it and let him learn this one his own."

"They were going to kill him!" Alley shouted, her tears slowing as the rage took over in her heated cheeks. Brushing tears aside, her hand slammed down on the counter. "Jesus Christ, Spencer, do you really think I could stand by and let something happen to him?"

"How is he supposed to learn anything if you're constantly protecting him? He's twenty-seven. At some point, he has to fucking grow up!"

"So you're telling me if Lex came to you and was in trouble like this, you'd turn your back on her?"

"Lexi is different. She wouldn't do this shit."

"If she did, would you?"

I couldn't believe she didn't see the whole picture. "With as many times as we've bailed Cole out, yes, I would tell her it's time to learn a lesson. You're missing the fucking point. This is my family, and you went to my brother for help. How do you think that makes me feel?"

"This is something I'm never going to agree with you on. He's my son, and I can't turn away from him."

Shaking my head, I drew in a heavy breath and let it out slowly. "But you can turn away from your husband?"

"I didn't want to turn away," she had the nerve to say. "*You* forced me to."

"Well, then, if that's the way it is, I suppose there's nothing left to say, is there?"

"What would you have done then? Leave him in jail and let him get killed by those guys?"

"That's something you and I should have discussed, not you and Jameson. And then you two go and send him to rehab without even talking to me about it?"

"Jameson made the arrangements. I didn't, and Cole went straight to rehab." She said this as if I should be okay with it. "I didn't have a chance to say anything before it was done and I figured since he was safe and everything was okay for now, it wasn't worth mentioning."

"Wasn't worth telling me you went behind my back to decide what's best for our son with my brother."

"You keep bringing up your brother like it's some kind of betrayal. Jesus, he's been there for us through everything and constantly supporting us. If it wasn't for your brother, I wouldn't have a job, neither would you, or Lane for that matter. Think of what he's done for our family."

"I know exactly what he's done. Which is why for once I would love to make a decision for my family and not have it run through Jameson Riley."

"Oh Jesus, Spencer. You don't have to run everything through Jameson and you fucking know it. You're being dramatic."

"Am I?" I saw red. "Fuck this. I'm leaving. I can't be here with you right now."

"What do you mean you're leaving?"

Pacing the kitchen with my hands behind my neck, I needed to leave. *Now.* "I'm... I think we need some time apart." My words shook with thirty years of love for this woman, but annoyed she couldn't see past our son and what this was doing to the two of us. Our eyes met: apprehension in hers, confusion in mine. I didn't know what leaving meant. It couldn't mean divorce, could it? At that point, I didn't know but I wouldn't go on like this.

Upstairs, I grabbed a bag and some clothes knowing it was the off-season and I wouldn't be traveling to Charlotte much.

"Where are you going to go? We need to talk about this, Spencer. I was trying to do the right thing."

"Alley, you didn't do the right thing, and what's worse is you don't even realize it."

When I was out the door, the reality of the situation and what I was doing hit me, but it still didn't stop me from leaving.

AUTHOR ACKNOWLEDGMENTS

THIS BOOK WAS for the Racing on the Edge fans. You wanted more of Jameson and Sway, and I honestly thought it was necessary to get inside their head in these moments with Sway's cancer and Jack's death. I also wanted to give you some closure with Cole, and where his story might go in the future. As you can see, I've left some things open, and there may be more stories in the future or a spin-off series. I'm not sure at this point; I just know that for me, this family is my go-to family. I can't even tell you how many times I've read this series, and I wrote it.

I have plans for more Racing on the Edge. I can't let go of them! Check out my Facebook page for more info but I'm planning another book this winter from Arie and Rager.

Thank you to my husband and daughter for allowing me to live my dream of writing and my crazy idea to cut out sugar while writing a book. It was hell, but you stuck by me. I love you both so much.

Thank you to Becky with Hot Tree Editing. In the year that we've been working together, you've honestly transformed my writing into something I can be proud of and taught me so much about editing. Thank you for taking time with me and helping me blossom as a writer. Love you! Thank you so much for helping me understand past and present tense better!

Tracy Steeg, I can't tell you how much I appreciate what you've done for me with the covers and graphics. I love what you did with the re-design of the series.

Lauren, this book wouldn't have been possible without you getting inside their heads and pushing me to explore Cole more. Thanks for everything love!

Janet, Barb, Marisa, Shanna, Ashley's, Jill, Keisha and Rachel, thanks so much, girls.

To my reader group, thanks for being so excited about this release and wanting more of the Riley family. I love this family so much. Here's to years more exploring them!

MEET THE AUTHOR

SHEY STAHL IS a *USA Today* best-selling author, a wife, mother, daughter, and friend to many. When she's not writing, she's spending time with her family in the Pacific Northwest where she was born, and raised around a dirt track. Visit her website for additional information and keep up to date on new releases: www.sheystahl.com.

You can also find her on Facebook:

https://www.facebook.com/SheyStahlAuthor

Racing on the Edge

Happy Hour

Black Flag

Trading Paint

The Champion

The Legend

Hot Laps

The Rookie

Fast Time

Open Wheel

Pace Laps

Dirt Driven ~ (Release date: TBA)

Behind the Wheel ~ Series outtakes (Release date: TBA)

The Redemption Series

The Trainer

The Fighter

Stand Alones

Waiting for You

Everything Changes

Deal

Awakened

Everlasting Light

Bad Blood

Heavy Soul

Crossing the Line

Delayed Penalty

Delayed Offsides

Delayed Roughing (Release date: TBA)

Unforgettable Series

All I Have Left

All We Need (Release date: TBA)

The Torqued Trilogy

Unsteady

Unbearable (September 2016)

Unbound (January 2017)